WHEN HEARTS MEET

WHEN HEARTS MEET

sequel to

Where the Heart Leads

ANITA STANSFIELD

Covenant Communications, Inc.

Covenant

Cover painting *Irises* © Carol Harding

Cover design copyrighted 2001 by Covenant Communications, Inc.

Published by Covenant Communications, Inc.
American Fork, Utah

Printed in the United States of America
First Printing: October 2001

08 07 06 05 04 03 02 01   10 9 8 7 6 5 4 3 2 1

ISBN 1-57734-855-9

Library of Congress Cataloging-in-Publication Data

Stansfield, Anita, 1961-
    When Hearts Meet / Anita Stansfield.
        p.   cm.
    Sequel to: Where the Heart Leads
    ISBN 1-57734-855-9
    1. Widowers--Fiction. 2. Mormons--Fiction.
PS3569.T33354 W444 2001
813'.54--dc21   20010452154
                                    CIP

To all the good members of the Oklahoma Tulsa Mission
who are taking such good care of Elder Stansfield.
Thank you.

CHAPTER 1

Coming Home

Sterling, Utah —1902

Ethan Caldwell spurred the horse he rode to go a little faster. It wasn't the greatest horse, but it was the best he'd been able to afford, and he felt a freedom owning it he hadn't felt in years. It was a different kind of freedom that had helped him to make the decision to go back, and he felt suddenly anxious to see what had once been home—a place he had openly avoided for more years than he cared to think about.

As the terrain took on a distinct familiarity, Ethan felt an onslaught of nerves. He fought the habitual urge to have a drink, reminding himself that he'd not indulged in the temptation for more than a month now. And he was determined to keep it that way. The horrors of where drinking had gotten him were still painfully close, and he refused to go back. He had no job and practically nothing to his name, but he was determined to find employment, work hard, and start over. But the new beginning could only happen after he made the final stop on a journey of healing—one that ultimately led him back to where all the pain had begun. Back home.

Ethan slowed the horse, realizing the home he'd once lived in wasn't far, but just up the road over the next hill. His mind wandered back through the memories. He'd married Hannah in the temple, and he'd had a good job in the mines. Their home had been far better than the one he'd grown up in, and Hannah had kept it well. With the expected arrival of their first baby, he'd believed things were almost too good, that a man like him just didn't deserve so much happiness. Then the worst happened. Hannah had died, and the baby had gone with her. Instantly his world turned upside down. When he could find nothing to ease the pain of his loss, the drinking habit he'd set aside with Mormonism was quickly taken up again. His drinking eventually resulted in the loss of his job, and subsequently his home and everything he'd owned. A friend's uncle had taken him in, and he'd spent the past several years just struggling to cope and fighting against his benefactor's every effort to help him get his feet on the right path. It had taken a brush with death to show him what a fool he'd been. A rolling boulder had barely missed him—an incident he considered too strange to pass off as happenstance, and too close for comfort. A year ago he'd started going back to church, but he'd still been unable to keep from drinking. And now, through what he considered a series of small miracles, he had finally come to terms with the loss in his life, and he was determined to make a fresh start.

Ethan stopped on the crest of the hill and looked toward the home he'd shared with Hannah. Somehow he knew that just going there would help put the haunting memories to rest. Beyond the curving road and waving trees it was difficult to see the house, but he immediately knew that something was different—extremely different. Years ago he'd heard that someone bought it and fixed it up after it sat empty for quite some time, but he'd still expected it to look the same. It didn't.

Ethan trotted the horse forward until he got a good view of the house. It was considerably bigger. A fence had been added. There were more flowers. And it had a neater, more comely appearance than he'd ever been able to give it with the long hours he'd worked in the mines. He rode up to the gate and dismounted, giving the house a closer examination while he tethered the horse to the fence. He stepped through the gate and up the walk, hoping that whoever lived there would not find his simple request inappropriate. He was finding this less difficult than he'd expected, and he wondered if having the house appear so different made it easier for him to acknowledge the reality that life moved on. And for whoever now owned this beautiful home, life seemed to be going on well.

Ethan hesitated on the steps. The porch had been lengthened considerably. A swing hung at one end, and a little bench sat at the other. There were two doors; the one closest to the swing had a quaint little wood sign. He stared at the words: *Jon and Maddie Brandt and family.* The other door boasted a shiny metal plaque: *Jonathon P. Brandt, M.D.*

With Ethan's limited education, he knew he could never pronounce the names in front of him, but he knew what the M.D. meant. "A doctor," he whispered into the late autumn breeze. He took hold of the porch rail, feeling briefly unsteady. The irony was a little difficult to swallow. *Where was the good doctor when this home had really needed him?* His desire to knock on the door and just have a peek inside suddenly faded. He wanted a drink so badly that it almost hurt.

Ethan turned to go down the steps, only to be stopped by the sound of a door opening behind him. "May I help you?" a woman's voice asked. Her tone was kind and gentle. He took a deep breath and turned to see a young mother with a small boy beside her, and she was obviously pregnant. Her blonde curly hair was pulled back loosely.

"Uh . . ." he managed in response to her expectancy, "I just . . ."

"Did you need to see the doctor?" she asked gently. The little boy scampered away, as if his curiosity had been filled. "He'll be glad to help you, even if you can't afford it. We can work something out."

"Oh, no," he said. "I mean . . . I'm not needing any help, not that kind at least. I just . . . well . . ." He stepped back onto the porch and fidgeted with the hat in his hands. "The thing is that . . . I used to live in this house. And I just got a hankering to have a look at it and—"

"Of course," she said brightly. "You must be Mr. Caldwell."

"That's right," he said, feeling startled and strangely comforted all at once. "How did you know my name?"

"Well I grew up around here. I don't believe we ever met; I lived a rather secluded childhood. But I knew of you and your wife. I believe she passed away—oh, I'm so sorry . . ."

She looked hesitant, but Ethan nodded. He expected to feel upset at hearing it mentioned, but her tone was so perfectly compassionate; his pain felt assuaged by the acknowledgment that he'd been through something difficult.

"It's a pleasure to meet you, Mr. Caldwell," she said, extending her hand. "How nice of you to stop by. I've often wondered if you still lived around here. I'd heard you were with relatives somewhere in Sanpete valley. I've often wished I could talk to you. There are some questions I have that I think you could answer."

"Really?" he chuckled. He couldn't remember the last time that someone had been pleased to see him. "What kind of questions?"

She laughed softly and opened the door wider. "Won't you come in?" she asked. "We were just about to sit down and have some lunch. I hope you'll join us."

"Oh, no," he said. "I don't want to impose or—"

"If you were imposing, I wouldn't have invited you," she insisted. "Please. There's no reason to be concerned. My husband's right inside the kitchen."

"Thank you, ma'am," he said and stepped in, feeling as if he were somehow dreaming. "That sounds right nice." A quick glance told him the house looked nothing the same, but it had exactly the same feeling as it had had before Hannah's death. He followed the woman down the hall to the kitchen. It too looked completely different.

The woman's husband was seated at the table, reading from a book. Ethan figured the man and he were about the same average height, with the same brown hair, although their features were as different as night and day. The man looked up and smiled even before his wife said, "Jon, this is Mr. Caldwell, the man who once owned our home."

"Mr. Caldwell," he said, extending a hand. "What a pleasure. Forgive me for not getting up. I broke my ankle just a few days ago and I'm a bit indisposed."

Ethan stepped forward and offered a healthy handshake. "Not a problem," he said. Then he chuckled. "Not a problem for me, anyway."

They both laughed with him, and he decided he felt comfortable with the couple.

"Mr. Caldwell," the woman went on, "this is my husband, Jon Brandt. And forgive my manners, my name is Maddie."

"You must be the doctor," Ethan said to Mr. Brandt.

"That's right, but you should call me Jon. Have a seat."

"I asked Mr. Caldwell to join us for lunch," Maddie Brandt said as Ethan took a chair opposite the doctor.

"Oh, but I should wash up first," Ethan said, shooting to his feet again. Mrs. Brandt smiled and motioned toward the water pump. As he watched the water fall over one hand, then the other, more than a decade slipped behind him and he could almost believe that Hannah was there in the room. He closed his eyes and listened to the bustling noises of a woman setting lunch on the table, and he had to consciously remind himself of where his life had come to. He cleared his throat, and his head, before he turned to Mrs. Brandt and said, "Might I help with something, ma'am?"

"No, thank you," she said. "We can eat now."

Ethan sat again and inhaled the aroma of the fried potatoes and bacon set in front of him. He noticed the thick slices of bread on the table, and the butter and cooked vegetables that were laid out. He couldn't remember the last time he'd had something home-cooked that smelled so good. His friend's uncle wasn't much of a cook, and neither was he. They'd managed, but the meal before him already seemed like a bit of heaven.

The boy Ethan had seen at the door came noisily into the kitchen, along with a girl that looked close to the same size. They climbed onto their chairs, then became silent as they carefully eyed him.

"This is Mr. Caldwell," their mother said.

"Hello," they both said at the same time.

"Hello," he replied. "And who might you two be?"

"I'm Lizzy," the girl said. She looked at her brother as if to cue him, but he said nothing. She sighed and added, "That's Hansen. He's my brother. He's five and I'm six."

"It's right nice to meet you, Lizzy . . . and Hansen."

They both giggled as if they shared a deep secret. Ethan smiled and Mrs. Brandt sat down. As Dr. Brandt began to offer a blessing his suspicions were confirmed that the family shared his faith. Even though the majority of the people around there did, he figured it was nice to know for sure.

"So," the doctor said when they'd begun to eat, "this was once your home. It must seem strange being here now, with the way it's changed, and the time that's passed."

"Yes sir, it does," Ethan said. "You've made it look right nice." He pointed at the doctor briefly and said, "You're not from around here. I can hear it in your voice."

"All these years and I still can't hide it," he replied with a chuckle. "Actually, I'm from Boston. And I don't believe you're originally from around here either, Mr. Caldwell. I detect a bit of a drawl that doesn't ring true of born-and-bred Utahns."

"All these years and I still can't hide it," he repeated, and they all laughed. "Actually, I grew up in Arkansas. I was on my way through here when I was, oh . . . about fifteen, I reckon, going to California. I found myself stricken with a nasty fever and a good woman took me in; Mrs. Humphrey was her name. She was widowed; her children had either passed on or moved away. She let me stay, and I did my best to take care of her until she died. It was her uncle I've been staying with the last while, although he passed on recently." He figured that was all they needed to know for now, and he tried to steer the conversation away from himself by asking, "So, what brought *you* out here to settle in such a small town?"

"I came to visit my aunt—as coincidence would have it—on my way to California," he said, and they all laughed again. "It would seem we have something in common, Mr. Caldwell."

Ethan smiled as Jon went on. "I fell in love with the scenery about five minutes before I fell in love with Maddie." He smiled and took his wife's hand across the table, filling Ethan with a deep ache that he doubted would ever go away. He'd long ago stopped wallowing in misery and longing for something that he couldn't have, but there were still moments when the desire pained him. It should have been him sitting in this kitchen, holding his wife's hand across the table, entertaining a stranger for lunch.

"So, who might your aunt be?" Ethan asked, if only to distract himself.

"Ellie Jensen," he said, and Ethan slapped his knee in amusement.

"Well, I'll be. Ellie? Oh, dear sweet Ellie. Bless her heart. She sure tried to comfort me after I lost Hannah." Hearing his own words brush at what he was trying to avoid, he quickly turned to Mrs. Brandt and said, "You told me you grew up around here. Who did you belong to then?"

"My parents are Glen and Sylvia Hansen; they live between here and Ellie's."

"Of course." He laughed again, then something incongruous struck his memory. "But I thought they only had one child and she . . ." He hesitated, not wanting to sound rude.

"Couldn't walk?" she guessed with a smile. He nodded, feeling a little embarrassed. But she laughed softly and he felt completely at ease. "That was me. But the problem was corrected. As you can see, I manage it just fine now."

"That's amazing," Ethan said, thinking he'd like to hear more of the story, but he didn't want to be nosy. The children asked to be excused and ran up the stairs. Ethan was amazed to realize that there actually were stairs. The house had only been one story when he'd owned it.

"This is the best food I've tasted in years," he said firmly. "I'm mighty grateful, ma'am. I must confess I was awful hungry."

"We're so glad you're enjoying it," Mrs. Brandt said. "Eat all you want. There's plenty."

Ethan nodded and indulged in enjoying more of the meal. He reminded himself that he was in the presence of fine, educated people, and he did his best to behave politely. Following some silence, he said, "You said you've got some questions for me. You've got my curiosity raised up like the hair on a scared cat."

The couple chuckled, and he wondered if his lack of education and lowly upbringing were evident to these fine people. Either way, it was evident they still accepted him. He couldn't help but like them.

"Well," Maddie said, "I knew very little about you and your wife, but living in this home, I've often found myself wondering what her life might have been like here. It might sound silly, but there have been a few times when I could almost believe that she was here with me."

Ethan didn't realize he was staring at Mrs. Brandt until she gently said, "I'm sorry. Perhaps it was insensitive of me to bring it up that way. I know her death must have been terribly difficult for you."

Ethan glanced away and cleared his throat. "Well, yes . . . but . . . well, no you're not being insensitive, ma'am. I just . . ."

When he couldn't come up with words to explain what he was feeling, he was relieved when she said, "Perhaps we could talk another time."

"Perhaps," he said. While the idea of getting to know these people better greatly appealed to him, he felt certain it wasn't likely to happen. Forcing a change of subject, he said to them, "I really do like what you've done with the place. You added on quite a bit. Real nice. It looks real nice."

As they talked for a few minutes about the added rooms which provided a separate clinic, Ethan once again found his mind wandering through memories. He was startled to hear Mrs. Brandt ask in a concerned tone, "Is something wrong, Mr. Caldwell?"

He forced himself to look at her. "Sorry, ma'am. My mind just got wandering." He glanced at Dr. Brandt and felt compelled to say what was on his mind. "It's just ironic, I guess, to see a doctor sitting in this room, when I once knelt on this very floor and wished with all my might that a doctor could have been here."

Ethan saw the concern on their faces before he realized that he shouldn't have allowed his thoughts to come out so openly. "Forgive me," he said. "I'm certain that you don't need to hear the—"

"On the contrary," Dr. Brandt said. "It's been my experience that talking through our struggles can be a good thing. I'm guessing you came here to make peace with your past. We're not going to judge your feelings one way or another. If you'd like to talk . . ."

Ethan chuckled tensely and eased his chair back a little. He wasn't exactly certain what made him feel so at home with these people, but it was easy for him to talk to them. "It happened right there on the floor . . . by the stove." He pointed absently, feeling as if someone else was talking. "One minute she was standing there, stirring and singing, the next she was curled up on the floor, crying and bleeding all over the place. She said the baby was coming, and she kept telling me that everything was going to be all right. I'd never seen a baby born before, but I knew it was too soon, and I knew it wasn't right. I wanted to go get a doctor, but there wasn't one close. It would have taken me hours to get to one and back, even on the fastest horse. She died right there in my arms."

Ethan listened to the silence following his little speech. He heard echoes of his own words circle around his mind, and he was amazed he'd been able to say all of it without falling apart and groping for a drink. He actually felt calm and in control. He must have come far.

He was startled from his thoughts by a loud sniffle, and looked up to see Mrs. Brandt wiping her eyes with the corner of her apron. "No need to cry for me, ma'am. It's been rough, I'll give you that. I got to drinking, and that's why I lost the house and such, but the Lord's been good to me in spite of my shortcomings, and I think I'm finally using the good sense He gave me to get my life back on the straight and narrow. I've been without a drink for more than a month now. I've got nothing to my name but a tolerable horse and a change of clothes, but I'm looking to get me a job, and then we'll just see what life brings."

Ethan chuckled self-consciously when he realized he was rambling. "Listen to me going on and on. You folks have been good enough to share your meal, and I'm mighty grateful for that. I've enjoyed visiting with you and I appreciate your time. I wonder if you might have something I could do to return the favor, you being slowed up with that bad foot and all." He nodded toward the doctor's foot.

"Well," they said in unison, exchanging a long glance as if they could read each other's minds. He remembered feeling that way about Hannah and the ache returned. But it felt healing to accept the pain and acknowledge what he felt, rather than try to drown it in a bottle of whiskey.

"Actually," Dr. Brandt said, "there are a few things that I can't do with this foot. Maddie's been managing, but I worry about her doing too much with the baby on the way. My uncle, Dave Jensen—Ellie's husband, I'm sure you know him?"

"Yes, I remember," Ethan answered.

"Well, Dave comes to help when he can, but since his boys went off to school, he's having trouble keeping up with his own work. I was helping *him* when this happened. Would it be too much to ask if you could just see that our animals have what they need? They were fed this morning, but the cows didn't get milked, and the eggs haven't been gathered, and the horses could use some attention."

"I'd be happy to, Dr. Brandt," he said eagerly, appreciating that he was needed.

"And," Mrs. Brandt said, "if you could pull a few weeds in the garden, we'd love to have you for supper as well. I've been intending to get to it with this lovely fall weather holding out, but with Jon laid up, there's just been other things that needed doing."

Ethan jumped at their generous offer. Work in exchange for food. It was a deal he could appreciate given the present circumstances. "If supper's half as good as lunch, it would be a pleasure," he said. "In fact, I'll get right on it. And thanks again for lunch."

Ethan found the barn in good order, and it was easy to find what he needed and figure out what should be done. Caring for animals and weeding gardens was something he'd grown up doing. He couldn't help recalling how this had once been his barn, with his animals in it. But rather than feeling envious of these people, he felt a deep gratitude for the opportunity to sort the past out from the present.

The afternoon sun warded off the subtle chill that had teased the morning air. Ethan enjoyed cool water from the well at the high end of the garden, and he found the weeding a pleasant task. He occasionally saw the children in the yard and laughed at their antics. He wondered how many children he and Hannah might have by now if she'd lived, but then he reminded himself to keep his mind in the present. As the sun moved toward the mountains in the west, Ethan looked at the neat garden rows of late vegetables, now void of any weeds, and felt gratified with the work he'd done. He turned to see Mrs. Brandt standing a short distance away.

"It hasn't looked that good all summer," she said. "It's evident you know how to work."

"Yes, ma'am, I do," he said. "I believe I forgot for a few years there, but it's coming back to me."

"Supper's on in a few minutes if you want to wash up," she said. "Just come on through the kitchen door and leave your boots on the porch. You're welcome to stay the night in the room behind the clinic, if you like."

"Thank you, ma'am," he said. "I'd be most grateful."

She smiled and turned toward the house as she called her children, "Hansen, Lizzy, Supper! Come and wash up."

Ethan found supper enjoyable as the children talked about their day. Seeing Jon and Maddie Brandt interacting with their children assured him they were good people. When the meal was finished, Ethan rose from the table and said, "Could I help with the dishes, ma'am?"

"No thank you, Mr. Caldwell. Hansen and Lizzy are learning how to wash dishes, and they're doing a fine job of it."

"However," Dr. Brandt said, "we'd love to have you join us for scripture study once the dishes are finished."

Ethan chuckled and resisted the urge to pinch himself. This day was just turning out too good to be true. He enjoyed every minute of listening to Dr. Brandt read from the Book of Mormon, and the sweet spirit that seemed to surround this good family. They invited him to join them for family prayer as well. Kneeling with them in a little circle in the parlor, Ethan felt at peace as Lizzy took his left hand and Hansen took his right. They both smiled up at him before they bowed their heads and the doctor offered a fine prayer.

Ethan was already feeling overwhelmed with gratitude when he heard the words: "And thank You, Lord, for sending Mr. Caldwell to assist us at this time. We ask Thy blessings to be with him, that his life might be good."

After the amen was spoken, Ethan couldn't keep himself from thanking the couple for everything they'd done. Fearing he might get emotional, he quickly added, "I'll just turn in now, and you can plan on me taking care of the animals in the morning before I set out. I appreciate your generosity and—"

"Do you have somewhere you need to go?" Dr. Brandt asked.

"Well . . . not really, no, but . . ."

"If you're looking for work, Mr. Caldwell, we could sure use you. We can offer you room and board, and pay you a small salary as well. It sure would get us through a rough time, and perhaps it would help you get by until you can find something more permanent."

Ethan swallowed carefully, fearing he might cry like a baby if he wasn't careful. "I'd like that very much. Thank you, sir. I can do whatever you might need me to do. I'm not afraid of hard work."

"Yes, that's clear," the doctor said, extending his hand as if to seal their agreement. "And please, call me Jon."

"Okay . . . Jon," he said and accepted the handshake. "Call me Ethan."

They exchanged smiles and Ethan took the lamp that Mrs. Brandt held out for him. "There's an outside door to the room," she said. "You should find everything you need. If you don't, please let us know."

"Thank you, ma'am," he said.

"Maddie," she corrected and smiled again. She had the brightest smile he'd ever seen.

"Yes, ma'am," he answered, and she laughed softly.

"Good night, Ethan," she said. "Sleep well."

"You too, ma'am. And thank you again."

Ethan easily found the door to this room. He entered to find it much finer than he'd expected. There were two single beds, a small sofa, a couple of small dressers with drawers, and a large closet with shelves. Another door was locked, so he figured it went into the clinic. He reasoned that the room was likely for medical patients who needed to stay and be looked after.

Ethan sat on one of the beds and pressed a hand over the fine, tightly crocheted blanket that was spread over it. He thought through the happenings of the day, then he got on his knees and thanked the Lord for guiding him there. In the midst of his prayer it occurred to him that the urgency he'd felt about heading back to his old home had not been for the sake of coming to terms with his memories—although doing so had certainly helped. Coming here had brought the answer to his every prayer. He had a place to stay, plenty to eat, and work to keep him busy and give him a fresh start. He gratefully crawled beneath the covers, certain he'd never had a bed so comfortable.

"Thanks again, Lord," he said toward the ceiling, and quickly drifted to sleep.

Ethan woke with the cock's crow and quickly got to work. The animals were all fed and cared for when he got to the kitchen door with one bucket of fresh milk, and one with several eggs. He was about to set one of them down and knock when the door came open. Maddie gasped quickly, then laughed.

"Didn't mean to startle you, ma'am," he said. "Where would you like me to put the milk and eggs?"

"Oh, my," she said, seeming surprised. "I was just going to come and wake you, and here you've already—"

"No need to wake me, ma'am. Where would you like these?"

"Oh, right here is fine," she said, motioning toward the counter beside the sink. "I'll have breakfast on in about half an hour."

Ethan set the buckets down. "Unless you got something else you want me to do," he removed his hat and turned the brim in his fingers, unsure of himself, "I'll start pulling those weeds along the west fence."

"Uh . . . that would be fine," she answered, smiling. "I'll ring the triangle when the food's on the table."

"Thank you, ma'am," he said and hurried across the yard.

At breakfast Jon proposed another chore. "Ethan, I wonder if you'd mind going into town for us and picking up a few things we need. I'll make you a list."

"I'd be happy to," Ethan said, feeling as if he were lying.

He was surprised at Jon's perceptive abilities when he was asked, "Is there a problem? If there is you need to speak up."

"Well . . . I've never been prone to hiding it," Ethan said. "It's just that . . . my reading . . . doesn't amount to much. If you'd make a list that I could give to the storekeeper, I can get what you need."

He noticed a subtle glance pass between the couple, but they both smiled warmly at him as Maddie said, "That's no problem, Ethan. We'll prepare a list as soon as we're finished eating."

Ethan nodded and cleaned his plate. He thanked Maddie for the breakfast and went back to do some weeding until the triangle rang. When he returned to the house, Jon met him at the back door, leaning on a crutch.

"Here's a list for Sister Larson at the store, and here's the money to pay for everything." As Ethan took the money Jon added, "You won't be buying any liquor with that now, will you."

"No, sir," Ethan said firmly, but Jon chuckled. Ethan glanced up and realized Jon was teasing him. He forced out a little laugh, not certain if he found it funny or not.

"Sorry about that," Jon said with a kind smile, his sincerity obvious. Ethan returned the smile, and found no reason to take offense.

"Also," Jon added, "would you pick up our mail for us? I'm sure you know your way around town."

"I'd be happy to," Ethan said, "but seeing that nobody in town knows I'm back, or that I'm working for you, would they be willing to hand over your mail?"

Jon's brow furrowed. "Good point," he said. "Hold on just a minute." He hobbled to the table and sat to write something on a piece of paper, which he then held out toward Ethan. As he stepped forward to take it Jon said, "Just give that to Sister Nelson at the post office. You shouldn't have any trouble."

"Thank you, sir. I'll hurry right along, then."

"No, thank *you,* Ethan. And my name is Jon."

"Yes, sir—Jon," he said, and Jon shook his head in amused defeat.

"Oh, and this afternoon, I wonder if you could go and help Dave, my uncle. He's trying to get some fences repaired in his north field. I'd be helping him if I wasn't laid up, business being a little slow for me at the moment."

"I'd be glad to," Ethan said, liking the thought of helping Mr. Jensen. His memories of the Jensen family were good to say the least.

"Hurry along," Jon said. "You don't want to miss lunch."

"No, sir, I don't. Your good wife is a mighty fine cook."

"Yes, she is," Jon said and Ethan hurried out to harness the wagon.

It was a beautiful day, and Ethan enjoyed the ride to town. He stopped the wagon in front of the store and went in. He found that Sister Larson was the only one in the place.

"May I help you?" she asked, looking at him inquisitively.

"Yes, ma'am," he said. "I'm here for Dr. Brandt. He sent this list and some money. If you could help me get what he wants, I'd be most obliged."

Sister Larson took the list and squinted at him before she said, "Ethan Caldwell? Is that you?"

He couldn't tell if she was pleased or disgusted, so he just said, "Yes ma'am, it's me."

"Well, you're looking a lot better than the last time I saw you, but that would have been years ago. Are things going better for you now?"

"Yes ma'am, they are." Almost hoping she'd pass the word of his return along, he took the opportunity to add, "I finally had the sense to quit drinking, and the good Lord's blessed me for it. Dr. Brandt gave me a job, just temporary while he's got that bad foot."

"Well, that's real nice," Sister Larson said. Then he followed her around while she gathered the items on the list. He gave her the money Jon had given him, and she gave him back some change.

"Thank you much, ma'am," he said, readying to leave the store with a box full of goods.

"It was a pleasure. You tell the good doctor to stay off that foot now, and I'll plan on seeing you in church on Sunday."

Ethan couldn't keep from grinning. "Yes, ma'am, I'll be there."

At the post office, Sister Nelson wasn't quite so friendly. She didn't say a word, but her expression made it clear that Dr. Brandt was a fool to hire a drunk, especially one who couldn't read or write worth a bean. He just thanked her for the mail and went on his way. He knew he couldn't expect to be working and living in *this* town without some people judging him. He'd behaved horribly before he left. He just had to hope that one day people would forgive him. Or maybe, once the Brandts didn't need him any more, he'd just move on to a place where no one knew him. Either way, things were still looking up and he was grateful.

"Here's your groceries, ma'am," Ethan said, setting the box on the table in front of Maddie. "The mail's there in the box next to the sugar." He reached into his pocket and set the change on the table. "And there's the money that's left."

"Thank you, Ethan. I hope you know what a blessing you are to us, an answer to our prayers, really. We just weren't sure how we would manage."

"Glad to do it, ma'am," he said. "I was thinking it was the other way around. I mean . . . I think I'm the one having my prayers answered, ma'am."

"Maddie," she said with that bright smile of hers. "My name is Maddie."

"Yes, ma'am," he said as he went outside.

"Lunch will be on soon," she called. "I'll ring the triangle."

"Yes, ma'am," he called back, and he heard her laugh.

CHAPTER 2
Running West

Ethan had been with the Brandt family four days when a telegram arrived. They were all sitting at lunch when a loud knock came at the front door. Maddie rose to answer it and returned with concern in her face.

"It's for you," she said, handing the envelope to Jon. "It's from Boston."

"Oh help," he murmured. "The last time I got a telegram from Boston my father was dying." He added, more to Ethan, "My sister and her family still live in Boston."

Ethan nodded and watched Jon hesitantly open the envelope and unfold the page inside. Jon's eyes scanned it quickly. He sucked in his breath, and Maddie put a hand to her heart.

"What is it?" she demanded.

When Jon looked up at her he had tears shining in his eyes. "It's from Sara," he said. "Harrison's been killed."

"Good heavens!" Maddie gasped, then pressed a hand over her mouth as she began to cry. The children looked concerned but said nothing.

"Harrison is my sister's husband," Jon said to Ethan, and he nodded in answer.

"Does she say how? What happened?" Maddie asked, her voice tense with concern.

"It just says an accident," Jon told her. "She says not to come; she'll be writing soon. That's it."

"Maybe we should go anyway," Maddie insisted. "How can she face something like this alone?"

"She has Mona. You know how Mona keeps everything under control. Besides, I can't travel very well with this leg, and . . . well, we can pray about going, but I just don't think we should." Jon sighed and slumped visibly in his chair. "I can't believe it. I can't even imagine what she must be going through."

"I can," Ethan said quietly, hoping it wouldn't be out of line.

Jon looked at him with a penetrating gaze. "Yes, I believe you can," he said, his voice almost a whisper.

Maddie began to sob and hurried out of the kitchen. Lizzy followed after her. Hansen remained at the table looking glum, his food forgotten.

"Excuse me," Jon said apologetically, and took up his crutches to follow after his wife. A minute after he left the room Lizzy returned. Ethan could see she was trying not to cry. He followed his instincts and pushed back his chair, opening his arms.

"Come on over here, little lady, and tell me what's wrong."

Lizzy rushed toward him, bursting into tears just as her face met his shoulder. Seeing his sister's tears seemed to prompt Hansen. The boy's emotions came into the open, and he quickly found a place on Ethan's other shoulder.

"Now," he said when they'd both calmed down and he'd situated one child on each knee, "why don't we talk about what's got you so upset."

"Uncle Harrison died," Lizzy said.

"Did you know your uncle very well?" Ethan asked.

"I only met him once," she said shaking her head, "when they came out to visit last year. He doesn't like children very much. But Phillip is our friend. We write letters to him and he writes us back. Our mamas help us."

"Is Phillip your cousin?" Ethan asked, and Lizzy nodded. Hansen seemed content to keep his head against Ethan's shoulder and let his sister do the talking.

"How old is Phillip?" Ethan asked.

"He's almost six," she said. "His age is halfway between mine and Hansen's."

She started to sniffle again and Ethan asked, "So, what is it that makes you so sad?"

"Phillip's papa died."

Ethan was humbled by the child's empathy as he wiped her tears with his fingers. "You know," he said, "I once had a good friend named Mrs. Humphrey. She was kind of like the grandma I never had, even though she wasn't really old enough to be my grandma."

"You didn't have a grandma?" Hansen asked.

"No, sir. My grandmas both died before I was born."

"Did you have a mother and father?"

"Yes, I did. I had a good mama and a good papa. They raised me to do what's right and work hard, but we were awful poor, and I didn't get much schooling because I had to help my papa run the farm. After my mama died, my papa took to drinking too much, and I started doing it right along with him. Then he died, and I came out west looking for work. When I got sick, Mrs. Humphrey took me in. She didn't approve of my drinking, but she treated me real good anyway. But the thing I wanted to tell you is how Mrs. Humphrey used to read to me out of the Bible and the Book of Mormon. I couldn't read too good myself, but she'd read to me a whole lot. And I want to tell you something I remember her reading to me. I remember it from when I got baptized so I could be a Mormon too."

"I'm going to be baptized when I turn eight years old," Lizzy said proudly, distracted from her grief.

"Me too," Hansen added.

"That's great," Ethan said. "And when you get baptized, you make a covenant with the Lord. Do you know what a covenant is?"

"Isn't it like a promise?" Lizzy asked.

"That's right. But it's a two-way promise. If we do the part we promise, then the good Lord does the part He promises. Anyway, I remember Mrs. Humphrey telling me about that in the Book of Mormon. It says that if we want the Spirit of the Lord to be with us, we should mourn with those that mourn. Now, I know having someone you love die can be an awful hard thing."

"Did someone die that you love?" Lizzy interrupted.

Ethan swallowed carefully and said, "Yes, a number of people at different times, and some were harder than others. The point I'm trying to make is that it's okay to feel sad when someone dies. And right now, it's good for you to feel sad for your cousin Phillip, and to try to understand how he must be feeling. And it might be a good idea if you went and wrote him a letter to tell him how you feel; it might even make you feel better."

"I'm going to right now," Lizzy said.

"Me too!" Hansen said, and they both slipped off of his lap.

"Oh," Lizzy added, looking downhearted, "Mama probably doesn't feel like helping me right now. She's very sad. She said she needs to be alone. Would you help us write a letter, Ethan?"

Ethan hated to disappoint them. "I'm sorry, pumpkin, but I'm not so good at writing. I'm sure that in a while your mother will—"

"I'll help you," Jon said, and they all looked up to see him standing in the kitchen doorway.

"Will you, Papa?" Lizzy asked.

"Yes, of course. I need to write Aunt Sara a letter. We'll work on them together. Why don't you go get some paper from the desk while me and Ethan clear the table. But first, why don't you go pick some of those late-blooming roses out front for your mother. Be careful of the thorns."

The children excitedly left the room. Ethan quickly stood up and began gathering dishes, wondering why he felt uncomfortable. When nothing was said for a couple of minutes, Ethan decided just to clear the air. "I'm sorry if my talking to your little ones that way was out of line or—"

"No, of course not," Jon said, struggling to maneuver one crutch while he stacked some dishes.

"Why don't you sit down and let me do that," Ethan insisted, "before you end up dropping something and making a bigger mess."

"Yes, sir," Jon said with a twinkle in his eye, and Ethan laughed at him. But the joviality passed quickly. Jon sat down, and Ethan sensed his sadness through the remaining silence as Ethan cleared the table and washed the dishes.

"Ethan," Jon said.

"Yes, sir."

"I just wanted to thank you."

"For what?" Ethan asked, stopping long enough to turn and face him.

"Well, for a lot of things. You came when we needed you. You're honest, hard-working, pleasant company. But most of all I wanted to thank you for what you just taught my children. I came into the room with a prayer in my heart that I could help them understand how to deal with this. And my prayer was being answered before I even got here. So, thank you for being the kind of man who helps the Lord answer prayers."

Ethan felt stunned. Hot tears stung his eyes and he turned back to the sink while he tried to blink them away.

"Did I say something to offend you, Ethan?" Jon asked.

"No, sir," he said, managing a steady voice. "I've just . . . never been the answer to somebody's prayers before. And given the paths I've been down the last several years, it's just nice to know."

"Well, good. But I bet you have."

"Have what?" he asked.

"I bet you've been the answer to somebody's prayers before. You probably just didn't know at the time."

"Maybe," Ethan said, and he needed to add, "That works two ways you know. I know the good Lord guided me here. You've certainly been the means to answer *my* prayers."

"Well then," Jon said, "I guess everything's just going to have to be all right for all of us."

"Yes, sir, I guess it is."

"My name is Jon."

"Yes, sir, I know."

"Call me Jon."

"Yes, sir, Jon," Ethan said, and they both laughed.

Just as Ethan finished drying the dishes, the children came in with a rose in each hand. He found a quart jar in a high cupboard, and Jon helped the children arrange the roses in it. Then Ethan went back out to the yard and resumed his work. An hour later Jon gave him three letters and a telegram to take to town.

The family said nothing more of the death in his presence, but Ethan sensed their grave moods, and he knew they were struggling. He suspected the distance they were from Jon's sister made them feel helpless. He couldn't help thinking about her and wondering what she might be like. He suspected she was a fine lady, educated and refined. Nothing like him. But in having lost his wife, he almost wished he could write her a letter himself and let her know what he'd learned—the hard way. But even if he could write worth a darn, he felt relatively certain she wouldn't have any interest in what a simple man like him would have to say.

On a rainy day, when Jon was extremely busy in the clinic, Maddie put Ethan to work with some heavy cleaning in the kitchen.

"It just gets so dirty around the stove and such after a while," she said, "and I'm just not up to all that scrubbing."

"You shouldn't be doing that kind of work in your condition anyway," Ethan said. "I'm glad to help."

She surprised him a few minutes later by asking, "Tell me about her, Ethan." He looked up and she clarified, "Tell me about Hannah."

Ethan started by telling her about the first time he'd seen Hannah. It was at a barn dance he'd gone to after helping put up somebody's barn. His work slowed as he talked about their courting, their marriage, and how he'd been able to buy the house. Then he found himself sitting on the floor as he repeated the events of her death, and how he'd fallen apart afterwards. Just as the first time he'd told her on the day he'd arrived, Maddie cried silently. But Ethan found that just watching her cry for him somehow soothed his wounds; it made him feel a little closer to being healed from the heartache that had torn his life apart. He wished he could find the words to express how much he appreciated Maddie's interest in his life, and her compassion on his behalf. But they shared warm smiles as she squeezed his hand, and somehow he knew she understood. Setting back to work, he realized that he actually felt happy.

* * * * *

Sara Hartford took the envelope from Mona's outstretched hand. The housekeeper gave her a concerned smile and Sara wondered what she would have ever done without her. Mona was like a member of the family.

"Thank you," Sara said, and put her attention to reading the telegram after Mona left the room. Her eyes misted over, and she had to blink several times before she could focus on the words in front of her.

Our hearts are with you. We should be together. Consider coming. Letter on the way. Jon and Maddie Brandt.

Sara looked toward the window and sighed. The simple words of the telegram strengthened an idea that had been teasing the back of her mind for a long time. But still, it seemed so preposterous, so drastic.

"I should stop thinking about it and just do it," she said to the empty room, wondering when she'd taken to talking to herself. She feared if she didn't get out of there soon she'd lose her mind.

Sara constantly thought about it while she waited for her brother's letter. Phillip was thrilled with the letter from his cousins. She read it aloud with him, and even though they both cried a little, she could tell that it made him feel better.

"I wish I could see Lizzy and Hansen," he said, adding more support to her thought that leaving was the right thing to do.

"I wish you could too," she said, not wanting to tell him her thoughts until she was more prepared to go. "You run along now and help Mona put lunch out while I read my letters."

Phillip did as he was asked and hurried from the room. Sara pushed a hand through her wavy dark hair and sat on the floor, pulling her knees to her chin to read what her brother and sister-in-law had written. Their letters were full of the comfort and hope she deeply needed, even though they had no way of knowing the full measure of her grief—and guilt. The last paragraph of her brother's letter suddenly made everything she'd been feeling perfectly sensible.

. . . We should be together, Sara. My heart is aching for you. We're family, and I want to be able to help you through this. I know how much the house means to you, and it has to be your choice, but I'm offering you a home here with us. Maddie and I have talked it over extensively. We have plenty of space, and the children would get along well. You could help me in the clinic, and we could help you get that baby here safely. Consider coming, even if it's temporary. And if you like it, maybe you'll decide to stay. Please let me know, and remember that you're in our every prayer.

With love and affection,

Jonathon Phillip Brandt

Sara read the last paragraph over three times, then she tossed the letter to the table beside her and hurried to the door. "Mona," she called, and the housekeeper came bustling up the stairs.

"What is it, dear?" she answered with concern. She was a full head shorter than Sara, with reddish-brown hair that never stayed in place, and she was full of a constant energy that made Sara tired just watching her.

"I've made a decision. I'm going to Utah."

"To visit your brother?" she asked eagerly, as if she also knew this would be good for Sara.

"Not exactly. It's difficult to explain, but . . ." She searched for a simple explanation, words that would help Mona understand without burdening her with unnecessary details. "It's as if this house is suddenly full of memories that are causing me more grief than good. I feel like I have to get away. I have to put it all behind me." She bit her lip. "What do you think, Mona?"

"I think it's a splendid idea. It would be good for you, and for little Phillip, too. I'll miss you terribly, but—"

"Oh, no Mona. I couldn't go without you. I guess that's what I want to know. Would you be willing to come with us? Would you consider it? I know you have no family connections here, but you've always lived in Boston. I know I'm asking a lot, but . . . it would just be so much nicer if you—"

"Don't even ask me twice!" Mona said with a little laugh. "I'd love to go. I've got a rather adventurous spirit, if you must know. As a girl I dreamed of going west, but it never worked out that way. And I'd sure be brokenhearted to lose you and Phillip." She laughed again. "We'd do well to get packing. We don't want to be traveling too close to that baby's expected time. I'll dig out the luggage and be on it right soon."

Sara heard herself laugh, something she'd not done since long before Harrison's death. Then she sat to write a quick note to her personal attorney. If she was going to make this work, she would need his help.

* * * * *

Sara watched her attorney pace back and forth in the study of her home.

"This is madness, I tell you. How can you just up and sell the house? Everything? To what? Settle in some stinky little town out west? Have you gone mad?"

"Listen to me Geoffrey, you've been a friend for many years. You've always done well for us, but I know I'm doing the right thing."

"How can you be sure when you're grieving? You can't make a decision like this when you're grieving. You've been asking my advice for years, and I'm advising you that this is not a good idea."

"You've been advising me in business and financial matters, Geoffrey, but this is a personal decision. I'm not asking for your advice. I'm asking you to see that my home gets sold for a fair price, and to help me transfer all of my affairs to Utah. And I expect to personally oversee every transaction, just as I always have."

"Are you saying you don't trust me?"

"It has nothing to do with trust, and you know it. My father always taught me to remain abreast of everything that has my name on it. You know that. So don't start questioning my judgment now. And I have to add that my grief for my husband's death is something that you know absolutely nothing about. I know the two of you were good friends, but you have no idea what's going on in my head, or my heart. So, will you help me, or should I find another attorney who won't think he has the right to run my life?"

Geoffrey looked at her as if her hair had turned green. "I've never seen you like this, Sara. I'm concerned for you. I would hate to see you do something so drastic, and then come to regret it later. What if you decide to come back?"

"Then I'll buy a different house. But I really believe that's where I want to be. I've been there before. It's not like I'm treading into unknown territory."

"All right, but . . . I fear you're just running away. You can't run from your problems, Sara."

Sara chuckled as she recalled saying those very words to her brother several years ago, the day he'd left to go west. His leaving here had turned out to be the best thing that ever happened to him, in spite of the difficulties he encountered. She recalled what he'd said to her then: *I'm not running away. I'm the one with enough self-respect to know that staying would only make a bad situation worse.* And that's where her life had gone—from bad to worse. She hadn't been able to see it back then, but she could see it now. And it was time she left Boston, knowing intuitively that she would never find her true self as long as she stayed where she had always been.

Sara looked Geoffrey firmly in the eyes and said, "I'm not running. I just know this is what I have to do. Now, do I have your support or not?"

"Yes, of course," he said, however begrudgingly. "I just hope you know what you're doing."

Sara looked toward the window and added silently, *So do I.*

Through the following days Geoffrey proved his efficiency in getting everything arranged for her, even beyond the call of duty. And Mona oversaw their packing with the common sense and competence that she was known for. Phillip's excitement rubbed off on her, and she found herself anticipating the journey to Utah—counting down the hours.

The day before they were scheduled to leave, Mona found Sara in her bedroom. With an expression that put Sara on edge, Mona set a rolled-up paper down on the bureau in front of Sara.

"What is this?" Sara asked.

"That's what I'd like to know," Mona said. "You know I've been giving the house a thorough check, wanting to find anything that might be of personal value to you."

"Of course," Sara said, baffled that Mona needed to explain something so obvious. "Well, I found this in the china closet behind the silver."

Sara's heart quickened with dread. Her suspicions concerning her husband's business dealings rose again. She knew practically nothing about the scandal, and wondered if it was better that way. Still, she couldn't resist unrolling the paper in front of her to see what it might be. She was surprised to see a partial map of the world, with places in India and China highlighted. Rolled inside the map were a few other papers with financial figures on them. She quickly rolled them back up, handing them to Mona as if they might burn her.

"Get rid of them," she said, then added as an afterthought, "Actually, send for that detective, Mr. Saunders, and give them to him—personally. Don't let anyone else see them."

"Of course," Mona said and left the room.

Sara forced her mind away from the discovery, just as she had ignored Harrison's strange behavior that eventually led to his death. She was going west to make a fresh start, to put all of that behind her once and for all.

The following day as they boarded the train, Sara had no thought beyond her destination. She hoped the letter she had sent to Jon several days ago would get there before she did. Either way, she'd manage. She knew in her heart she was doing the best thing she could possibly do with her life. It was time to start over, and, God willing, it would be a good start.

* * * * *

Ethan went into the back door of the clinic. He knew Jon would be there, since he'd had a couple of appointments that morning, and a child needing stitches had shown up with his mother just before Ethan left for town. He liked the comfortable routine they'd developed throughout the last few weeks, and he liked the way the Brandts' influence was rubbing off on him. He'd realized early on what a golden opportunity it was for him to spend so much time with such people. He'd completely lost his urge to drink, feeling so much security in the structure of their lives. And he'd made a conscious decision to pay attention to their example and be more aware of his manners and speech. He'd never liked the way his lack of education came through when he talked, and he was quickly learning to remedy that. Although he doubted he'd ever be able to get rid of his Arkansas drawl. And that was okay, he concluded. This was not about changing who he was; it was about trying to better himself in order to find a better life.

"Hello, Ethan," Jon said, leaning on one crutch while he put medical instruments in a container of disinfectant. Jon had shown Ethan around the clinic a little, explaining a few things here and there. Ethan found it all fascinating. He couldn't even imagine the knowledge in Jon's head, and he felt privileged to have such a friend. That's how he thought of Jon; he knew that no matter how short a time he might be there, Jon Brandt would always be his friend.

"Got it all taken care of?" Ethan asked, seeing that everyone had gone.

"Nothing too serious," Jon said. "It's been a rather slow morning actually. What have you got there?"

"Oh, it's a letter from your sister. I brought it straight here, knowing you'd be anxious."

"Yes, thank you," Jon said and sat down. He groaned as he put his foot up and took the letter.

"Foot giving you grief?" Ethan asked.

"It's not horrible, but I can sure tell when I've been up and around. It does better when I stay off it and keep it elevated."

"Then you'd better do just that," Ethan insisted.

"Yes of course, Doctor Caldwell," he said and Ethan laughed loudly.

"Now, that's really funny," Ethan mused aloud. "Whew. Imagine that." Jon chuckled and opened the envelope.

"Can I help here?" Ethan asked, noting the blood-soaked rags and blood on the table.

"Yes, thank you," Jon said. "You can throw the rags in that bucket to soak. And wash your hands good when you're finished."

"Yes, sir," he said and Jon chortled again. It had become a common joke between them, which allowed Ethan to comfortably call Jon *sir*. In spite of their growing bond, he had a hard time calling Jon anything else when he was still the man's employee.

Jon read silently while Ethan did his best to clean up the mess. He was startled when Jon said abruptly, "Good heavens!"

"What?" Ethan retorted. "Somebody else didn't die, did they?"

"No, but—what's today, Ethan?"

"It's Tuesday, why?"

"Well," he laughed, evidence that the surprise was a pleasant one, "my sister is on her way here, with her son and Mona. Her train arrives Thursday morning. We'd do well to go tell Maddie and the children the news, and we're going to have to get the spare rooms aired out and ready."

"When you say *we* I know you mean *me*," Ethan laughed. "Mrs. Brandt hobbles almost as much as you do with that baby coming."

"Yes, you're right, Ethan. But *we* do well at supervising and giving orders, don't we? I hope you don't get too fed up with us."

"Never," Ethan smiled. "It's the best job I've ever had. Nothing personal, but I'm mighty thankful you broke that ankle."

Jon laughed. "When you put it that way, maybe I am too."

Ethan followed Jon through the door joining the clinic to the house. They found Maddie and the children sitting at the table cutting biscuits.

"Guess what?" Jon said, plopping himself into a chair and lifting his splinted foot onto another.

"What?" they all asked together.

Jon waved the letter and Maddie asked, "It's from Sara?"

"That's right, and she's going to be here the day after tomorrow."

Maddie let out a squeal of laughter that set off Jon and Ethan as well.

Lizzy asked excitedly, "Is Phillip coming, too?"

"Yes, he is," Jon said, and the children began jumping up and down, full of anticipation.

"And Mona is coming as well," Jon added. Then he looked at the children. "We need to all work together to get the spare rooms ready. We don't want your mother getting tired out, and you know my foot's not working too well."

Ethan enjoyed preparing for the great arrival, working right along with the family. For the first time he was able to see the full extent of how the house had been expanded. He'd noticed that there were two sets of stairs, one at the front of the main hall, and the other going up from the kitchen near the back door. Of course, when he'd lived in the house there had been no stairs at all, except for the ones going down to the cellar. Now he realized that the front stairs led to bedrooms and a bathroom for the family, while the stairs going up from the kitchen led to a bathroom and four small guest bedrooms that were completely separate from the family's living quarters.

"I've never been up here before," Ethan said as he peered into the rooms. Jon followed slowly on crutches.

"We tried to be thoughtful as we added on to the house," Jon said. "I got an inheritance from my father, and we wanted to be able to use it in a way that we could help people in need. So we added these rooms in case multiple patients needed to stay close by, or we can use them for guests—whichever might suit our needs. They've not been used often, but when they are, we're sure glad to have them."

"It's real nice," Ethan said. "Your sister ought to be mighty comfortable here. And her son, too. What's his name? Oh yeah,

Phillip. And that's your middle name, right?"

"That's right. My father's name was Phillip."

"And she's bringing Mona," Ethan recalled. "Who exactly is Mona?"

"A housekeeper technically, but I believe they've become very close." Jon looked around and sighed. "Yes, I hope they'll be comfortable here. Sara seemed to enjoy her stay here last year, but she's accustomed to a very different life." He laughed good-naturedly. "It could be interesting."

"Well," Ethan said, setting himself to work, "we wouldn't want it to be dull."

"No," Jon agreed with a wink, "we certainly wouldn't."

Ethan opened all the windows in each room to air them out a bit. Then, according to Maddie's instructions, he took the bedspreads off and shook them outside to get rid of the dust, and then he hung them on the line to air out. The rest of the bedding stayed since it had been put on clean and hadn't been used since. In order to have everything on hand to prepare meals, Maddie sent Ethan to town with a long list. He returned to find that Lizzy and Hansen had dusted and polished every possible corner according to their mother's direction. With the windows now closed, Ethan replaced the bedspreads and set to sweeping the polished wood floors.

"So, tell me Ethan," Jon said from where he sat on the bed watching, "if you could do anything in the world with your life, what would it be?"

"Ah," Ethan smiled to himself, "just to have a good wife and a few kids, and a good job that would keep everybody fed and happy. That would be good enough for me."

"I can appreciate that," Jon said. "But what I mean is, if you could have any kind of life—anything at all—what would it be?"

"Is this a trick question?" Ethan asked, pausing to study Jon's expression.

"No," Jon smiled, amused. "I'm simply making conversation. Just tell me."

"Well, if you must know, I thought about that a lot when . . . well, when I was drinking all the time. I thought if I could just stay sober, I would love to . . ."

"What?" Jon pressed when he hesitated.

"Nah," Ethan said, putting his concentration more fully on his sweeping, "it sounds mighty silly."

"What? You think I'd make fun of you? Just tell me." When Ethan hesitated still, Jon said, "Travel the world? Be a great politician? A banker?"

"Nah," Ethan answered, "what I would really love to do is . . . well, if I had enough money so that I didn't have to be working all the time, I'd just like to, well, help other people work."

There was a long moment of silence before Jon said, "I don't understand."

"Well, all my life I've seen people struggling for one reason or another, people who can't work because they get laid up, or hurt— kind of like you—or there's just too much work to do all at once. And I'd just like to be able to . . . help where I might be needed most."

When Jon said nothing, Ethan stopped and turned to look at him. "Sounds silly, doesn't it?"

"No, Ethan," he said in a voice that sounded almost emotional, "I don't think it sounds silly at all. I just think you're a good man with a big heart, and I'm glad to call you my friend."

Ethan sighed deeply. "I'm glad to call *you* my friend."

He vigorously returned to his sweeping and Jon asked, "Then what's wrong?"

Ethan chuckled and shook his head. "I'd swear you read minds sometimes."

"It doesn't take a mind reader to see that something's eating at you. What is it?"

"Well," Ethan said, actually glad to have someone to talk to, "I have to wonder sometimes if . . . well, *if* I'm a good man with a big heart, why am I all alone . . . starting over . . . instead of having a wife and three or four kids? Now, don't get me wrong," he hurried to add, "I've been greatly blessed, and I'm not complaining. It's just that sometimes I wonder."

"I don't know, Ethan. Life can be rough sometimes, but I'd bet the good Lord has something in mind for you. Who knows? Maybe there's some incredible woman on her way into your life right now, but neither one of you know it yet."

Ethan chuckled. "Yeah, maybe," he said dubiously, and went into the next room to sweep.

On Thursday morning at breakfast, Jon said to Ethan, "I assume all the chores are done, as usual."

"Yes, sir," Ethan answered.

"Good. As soon as you eat, you can pick up my sister at the station while we finish up a few things here."

Ethan was taken aback. For the first time since he'd arrived, he was being asked to do something that he didn't want to do. Before he thought about what he was saying, he blurted, "Alone?"

Jon stifled a laugh. "That's what I had in mind. Is there a problem?"

"Well, I suppose not," Ethan said. "It's just that . . . I'd rather dig a ten-foot trench than go pick up your sister."

Jon laughed boisterously, though Ethan didn't see the humor. "May I ask why?" Jon questioned.

"Well . . . I'm just not so good with people. I don't even know her, but I do know she's a fine, educated lady, and I'm just . . ."

"Just what, Ethan?" Jon pressed, obviously not agreeing with Ethan's line of reasoning.

"Nothing," Ethan said, realizing this was a ridiculous conversation. "I'd be happy to pick your sister up at the station." He stood up and pointed at Jon. "But I get *your* piece of pie after supper."

* * * * *

Sara's heart quickened as the train drew to a grinding halt. She prayed that Jon had gotten her letter, and someone would be there to meet her. Somehow she knew the path to her future began when she stepped off this train. She stood on the platform, Phillip's hand in hers, searching for her brother. She turned to find herself face to face with a man who shared her brother's build and hair, but who looked nothing like him.

"Do I know you?" she asked tersely, not liking the way he stared at her.

"No, ma'am," he said. "But I know you."

"And how is that?" she demanded, looking him over carefully. He wore sun-faded overalls, over-worn work boots, and a hat that looked older than she felt. The drawl in his voice was unlike anything she'd ever heard in her life.

"You would be Mrs. Sara Hartford, and I am here to take you

home." He smiled widely and added, "Dr. Brandt sent me."

Sara was about to assert that she wasn't going anywhere with anyone except her brother, but upon really looking at the man, she decided she couldn't fathom him being anything but perfectly innocent and genuine. His returned gaze seemed to penetrate right through to her soul. She felt completely safe and wholly unnerved at the same time.

"If you'll direct me to your luggage, ma'am," he said, startling her from a near daze, "we'll be on our way."

"Of course," she said, and within minutes he had everything loaded and they were ready to go.

Ethan couldn't help smiling as Sara Hartford reluctantly put her hand into his as he helped her onto the seat. He'd expected her to be beautiful and elegant. And she was. He *hadn't* expected her to be significantly pregnant, although not as far along as Maddie, he figured. But that hadn't surprised him as much as the way he felt in her presence. In spite of his ongoing loneliness, he wasn't yet seeking out female companionship, and he certainly wasn't ready to feel even a glimmer of what he'd lost with Hannah. It only took him the few minutes of gathering their baggage to know that admitting to his attraction was preposterous. This beautiful young widow would no more take a second glance at him than she would a bullfrog. He felt somehow like he was in a fairytale, but he could never be the handsome prince—he was just a plain old frog, lucky enough to be near the princess for just a minute or two.

When Sara was comfortable, Ethan turned to help the middle-aged woman who had come with her. "You must be Mona," he said, taking her hand to help her up as well.

"I am indeed," she said brightly.

"It's mighty nice to meet you, Mona. I'm Ethan."

"Such a pleasure, Ethan." She said it as if she meant it.

"I'm Phillip," the boy piped in.

"Hello there, Phillip," Ethan said. They both climbed onto the seat and then started for home. "So," Sara began without looking at him, "why was Jon unable to come?"

"That would be mostly due to his broken ankle," Ethan said.

"*What?*" she exclaimed, as if she couldn't have heard him right.

"I didn't stutter, ma'am. It happened weeks ago."

"He said nothing about it in his letters," she insisted, as if she could somehow convince him that he was wrong.

"I'm sure he figured you had bigger worries on your mind. He manages to see his patients, but he doesn't get around real well, which is the biggest reason he's got me, just to see that the work's done until he can get around better. And of course, Mrs. Brandt's about to have that baby any day now, and he didn't want her to be going out."

"I didn't realize she was so close to her time," Sara said, the concern evident in her voice. "I hope I didn't cause an uproar, my coming with so little warning."

"Nah," Ethan said, "they're all just pleased as punch. Dr. Brandt wouldn't have invited you if he hadn't wanted you to come."

She said nothing more and he wondered where her thoughts might be. He wanted to ask but knew it wasn't his place. Little Phillip broke the silence with a string of questions. When his mother didn't seem inclined to answer them, Ethan did his best to tell the child why there were so many hills, why they couldn't see the ocean from here, and why some of the dirt looked red.

It started to rain before they arrived, but Ethan quickly alleviated Sara's distressed expression when he said, "Not to worry, Mrs. Hartford. I came prepared." He bent down to pick up an umbrella and handed it to her. She smiled and nodded appreciatively, but said nothing.

He brought out a second umbrella and handed it to Mona, who said, "Oh Ethan, you're truly a gentleman. Thank you."

"My pleasure, ma'am," he said. He glanced discreetly at Sara Hartford and decided this was much better than digging a ten-foot trench.

CHAPTER 3
The Distinguished Mrs. Hartford

Beyond carrying the luggage to the appropriate rooms, Ethan had no involvement in the happy reunion of the Brandt family. They were obviously all pleased to see each other, in spite of the cause for the visit—their shared grief. Dave and Ellie came by to join in the reunion, and it took Ethan a moment to recall how they were Sara's family. As always they greeted Ethan warmly, but Ethan sensed Sara Hartford's surprise at their attitude toward him, as if they should be disturbed by his presence as well. A little later Maddie's parents came by to visit. Glen and Sylvia Hansen were good people who always made Ethan feel welcome, but he left the family to their visiting and went about his business.

Since the rain drops were now coming in torrents, Ethan went to the barn and made himself useful by sharpening some tools and oiling a saddle. But in spite of every effort to keep it occupied, his mind was caught up with Sara Hartford. Even thinking about her seemed a fruitless endeavor. He tried to convince himself that her arrival was simply a big event, and he was naturally curious and caught up in the excitement. But something deep inside, something uncomfortable and fearful, knew there was more to his intrigue than that. And he knew it was impossible. It was ludicrous to think that he could be attracted to someone he'd barely met, and even more ludicrous to muse on the fact that he was.

He was startled to hear the barn door open, and he looked up to see Maddie, an umbrella in one hand and a covered plate in the other. "You must forgive me," she said. "We were halfway through lunch when I realized I'd not rang the bell to call you in. Just so much going on, I suppose. Anyway, here's some lunch for you." She smiled and held it out to him.

"Thank you, ma'am. You didn't have to come all the way out here in the rain. I'd have come in when I got hungry enough."

"I hope you would, Ethan," she said. "I hope you know that you're practically family, and you need to make yourself at home, in spite of anything that might be going on with us. If you need anything, Ethan—anything at all—please come and talk to one of us. Promise me."

Ethan felt almost dazed with humility and gratitude. Since his mother's death, as a boy of twelve, he'd had a few people who cared for him and took him in, but he'd never known such open concern and generosity. Her words echoed through his mind. *Practically family . . . make yourself at home . . . anything at all.* He forced words to his lips in response to her expectant expression.

"Yes, ma'am," he said. "Thank you."

She smiled, seeming terribly relieved. "I'll ring the bell for supper, Ethan. If you get hungry before then you know where the kitchen is."

"Thank you," he said again, and she went out. For the few seconds the door was open, he could see that the rain was every bit as hard as it had sounded on the barn roof.

Ethan felt the warmth of the Brandts' kindness and generosity as he ate his meal. He spent the afternoon finding everything he could do within the shelter of the barn. By the time the supper bell rang, the place was immaculate and everything in good repair. He took a long look around before he went out, satisfied with the work he'd accomplished. He stepped outside and was surprised to find that the rain had quit, and the evening sky was mostly void of clouds. The temperature in the air was not terribly unpleasant for November, as if the storm had been autumn's final farewell, rather than winter's first greeting.

Ethan removed his boots on the porch and set them just inside the back door. He went inside to wash and found Jon and the children seated, and the women putting supper on the table. The company had obviously left. He thought Maddie looked a little pale and was about to say so when he caught sight of Sara Hartford. One glance at her made his heart quicken, verifying something he'd been trying to talk himself out of.

"What have you been doing today, Ethan?" Jon asked lightly. "We've missed you."

"Just making myself useful out in the barn, trying to stay dry and busy at the same time."

"Very wise," Jon said.

Ethan greeted Lizzy and Hansen with some playful teasing as usual, then involved Phillip in the banter, not wanting him to feel left out. The newcomer giggled along with his cousins. Ethan greeted Mona as well, who responded warmly, then he nodded toward Sara and said, "Mrs. Hartford. I assume you're settling in well."

"Very well, thank you," she said and quickly turned her eyes away.

Ethan enjoyed the conversation at the supper table, preferring to listen rather than be involved. Jon and Sara reminisced about common memories. Maddie joined in as they talked about a trip they'd taken to Boston when Jon's father died. Lizzy had been born there.

When dessert was served, Ethan was surprised when Jon slid his piece of pie over to him. "What's this for?" Ethan asked, but Jon just grinned.

Ethan suddenly recalled demanding Jon's piece for going to get Sara. He was just about to tell Jon that he'd been joking when Lizzy asked, "Why are you giving Ethan your pie, Papa?"

"Oh, we had a deal," Jon said. "He had a rather unpleasant task to do earlier today, and I thought he deserved an extra piece of pie."

"No, that's all right," Ethan said, sliding the plate back toward Jon. "It didn't turn out to be too bad, after all. Either way, I wouldn't want to deprive you of a piece of Mrs. Brandt's apple pie."

Jon grinned and ate his pie, but there was something in his eyes that made Ethan wonder if he had an inkling of Ethan's feelings; that he felt terribly uncomfortable with Sara around, and at the same time just wanted to be in the same room with her. He certainly hoped not. Feeling this way was embarrassing enough. Having anybody know about it would be a disaster.

When the meal was finished, Ethan stood from the table and said to the little ones, "Why don't I help you children clear the table and wash up these dishes? We'll let the expectant mothers have a rest, and we all know your Papa's not worth anything with that bum foot."

The children giggled and hurried to help him. Mona helped as well, and they cleaned up quickly while Jon went with his wife and sister to the parlor. It was only when they all gathered for scripture study that Ethan realized Sara wasn't a member of the Church. And of course, neither was Mona. While Jon read from the Book of Mormon, Ethan's mind wandered back to the years of his life before he'd joined the Church, and he actually felt sorry for the women. He thought of his drinking and subsequent struggles over the years after he lost Hannah. He knew that his grief was for the lifetime they could have shared, but he'd always had an inner peace knowing that she was in a better place, and that eternity was real. He figured if he hadn't known what the gospel taught, he probably would have taken his own life rather than face the horror of losing Hannah. He couldn't comprehend how Sara might be dealing with her husband's death without knowledge of the gospel. He felt compelled to ask her, but knew it wasn't appropriate. He sensed a subtle disdain coming from her, and he wondered if she disapproved of him being so involved with the family. Or perhaps he didn't know her well enough to understand where she was coming from. Either way, he knew she would never give a man like him a second glance, and she certainly wouldn't think that anything he might share with her had any value.

Ethan had trouble sleeping that night. Thoughts of Sara Hartford wouldn't relent. He was angry with himself for feeling for her at all—and angry over a childhood and view of the world he'd never bothered to question before today. He finally slept with the firm resolve that within a few weeks he would be leaving here and he'd probably never see her again. His distress was temporary. He had faith that God had something good in store for his future as long as he worked hard and tried to do what was right. And he figured that the path to that future lay elsewhere—it just had to. Nothing else made sense.

* * * * *

Sara woke up for the first time in her new home. Though she recalled the time they'd spent there on a previous visit, she knew this was no visit. This was where she intended to stay. She wanted to be close to her brother. And Maddie was the sister she'd never had, the friend she'd never been able to find. It was perfect—the children got along well, and she felt safe and secure. And the suffocating feelings she'd endured in Boston seemed pleasantly distant—most of them, at least.

Sara's mind skimmed over the events that led to her current circumstances, and the decision she'd made to come to Utah. Her thoughts raced through memories of her husband's death and the subsequent funeral. She pondered briefly on the preparations for her journey, and the long train ride west. Then her mind seemed to come to a dead stop with the images of her arrival and coming face to face with Ethan Caldwell. When she couldn't make herself think of anything else, she reasoned that she was simply curious; she'd never known anyone like him—ever.

Sara got dressed and put up her hair before she went down to the kitchen. She entered to find that the children had all eaten and gone off to play. She hadn't even known that Phillip was awake. Jon and Ethan were sitting at the table, talking and laughing, while Mona worked at the sink, obviously involved in the conversation.

"Good morning," Jon said when he saw her. "You must have been tired. It's too late for breakfast; you'll have to wait for lunch."

"Don't you let him tease you," Mona said. "I've got your breakfast kept warm in the oven. You just have a seat and I'll put it on."

"Thank you, Mona," Sara said, sitting as far from Ethan Caldwell as possible. She couldn't explain why she felt so uneasy in his presence.

"How did you sleep?" Jon asked her, just as Ethan rose to his feet.

"Oh, don't leave," Jon said.

"I'm just going to make myself useful," Ethan said, and he started wiping the dishes Mona had just washed.

"Thank you, Ethan," she said. "You're a real sweetheart."

"As long as the good doctor keeps me fed, I'm willing to do almost anything," he answered.

"Almost," Jon said. "There are some things he won't do without the bribery of extra dessert."

Ethan and Jon exchanged comical smirks, then they both laughed before Jon turned back to her and repeated his question, "So, how did you sleep?"

"Very well, thank you. It's a nice room and a fine bed. I must say it feels good to be here."

"I'm glad," Jon said, "because it's good to have you here. I don't have to worry about you if you're here where I can take care of you."

Sara smiled and started to eat the breakfast in front of her. "Where's Maddie?" she asked.

"She's not feeling well," Jon said. "I'm afraid she's coming down with a cold. She's resting at the moment."

"You know, Jon," Sara said, "there's something I'd like to discuss with you."

"I'm listening," he said.

Sara wished they were alone, but Mona already knew what she had to say, and it certainly wasn't some great secret that should be kept from Jon's hired help. "Well, I didn't take the time to explain everything in my letter, but . . . I'm not going back to Boston."

"Really?" He seemed pleased. She figured that was a good start.

She sensed Mona and Ethan become quiet as they worked, and she hated feeling like she had an audience. "The thing is, I sold the house and . . . well, I sold practically everything." Jon's brows went up but he said nothing. "I thought it would take time to sell the house, but Geoffrey had a buyer right away, and everything went through very smoothly."

"Sounds like it was meant to be," Jon said.

Sara was relieved to hear her own feelings validated. "Yes, I believe it was. I really like it here, Jon. And I really appreciate your suggestion about helping you in the clinic some, just as I did with Father. I want to stay here, but . . ." She glanced toward Ethan when she realized what she'd almost said. Determined to bring up certain factors later, she pressed on in a different direction. "I love the rooms upstairs, and your hospitality is very generous, but I want to have my own home built. I was hoping you could help me. I want to buy a piece of ground, and hire someone to build me the place. Do you think that's possible, Jon?"

Jon laughed softly and put his hand over hers on the table. "I think it's one of the best ideas I've ever heard. In fact there's some property for sale just up the lane. We can go look at it and see what we can do. I know a fine builder. He's the one who added on to this home. We'll talk to him and see when he could do it. I believe he's in the middle of a job right now, but there's no big hurry. We want you to be with us until after the baby comes, anyway."

"Of course," she said, sighing with relief. Just knowing she could put down roots there made her feel that her past was truly behind her.

A little later, when Jon and Sara were alone, she felt compelled to admit some of her true feelings. "Jon, I really appreciate your giving me a haven here, more than you could possibly know."

"It's my pleasure, really. And once Maddie gets feeling better, I know the two of you will have a great time."

"Yes, I believe we will. I hope you don't think my coming here like this to make a fresh start—such a drastic measure—is too rash."

"I'm glad you're here, Sara. I'm glad you made the decision you did. But I get the feeling you're trying to tell me something else."

Sara looked at him and found some of her courage dwindling. She settled on telling him a portion of the truth. "I just feel the need to find myself, Jon. To put it succinctly, I woke up one day and realized that I'd spent most of my life trying to please a controlling father, and the rest of it trying to please a controlling husband." Jon sighed, more with concern than disgust, but she quickly added, "And don't say 'I told you so.'"

"I would never say that."

"No, but you have to be thinking it, because you *did* tell me so. I guess we both have that Brandt stubborn streak. We have to learn things the hard way."

"That's likely true," Jon said.

"I'm here, Jon, because I need to find myself. I need to learn who I really am, so that I can be truly happy. I had to leave my old life, my old home—everything—behind. Perhaps one of these days I'll be ready to get into the details of all that's happened. For now, I just want you to know that I'm grateful to have you and your family. I knew that I needed to be near my family. And that's why I'm here."

Jon smiled. He took her hand and kissed her cheek, and somehow she knew everything would be all right.

Jon went upstairs to be with Maddie, so Sara spent what was left of the morning wandering the house to acquaint herself, and toying with the piano.

"That's real nice music," she heard Ethan say, and turned abruptly to see him standing in the parlor doorway.

"Thank you," she said, avoiding his gaze.

A long moment later he said, "Mona sent me to tell you lunch is on."

"Thank you," she said again, and he walked away.

Sara entered the kitchen to see Ethan bouncing Hansen on one knee and Phillip on the other, while he made ridiculous horse noises that could barely be heard above the boys' giggling. She couldn't help smiling to see Phillip enjoying himself so thoroughly. Something ached inside of her to think of the father he'd lost, but the thought was immediately followed by the realization that he'd never really had a father in most respects. Harrison had never once played with Phillip, or even spoken to him beyond necessary exchanges. To see this man playing so openly with Phillip, provoking the boy's laughter and excitement, touched Sara deeply. But her pleasure was edged with a familiar guilt she couldn't deal with. By habit she stuffed the feelings down to where she could avoid them, and then seated herself at the table.

"Where's Jon?" Sara asked. Mona shrugged her shoulders, but Ethan looked up in concern as the boys reluctantly slid from his lap to take their seats by Lizzy.

"I'll go and find him," Ethan offered. He rose to his feet just as they heard Jon's crutches on the stairs.

He entered the kitchen looking upset.

"What is it?" Sara asked.

"Maddie's got a fever," he answered.

Sara rose to her feet. "I need to go see if she—"

"No," Jon said. "I know she would love to have you with her, but I'm not certain what it is. I don't want you exposed to it, especially since you're pregnant." He turned to Ethan and said, "Ethan, my friend, I'm going to stay with Maddie. I want to keep a close eye on her with the baby coming so soon. I wonder if you could watch the children and see that they have what they need, so that Sara doesn't tire herself too much."

"I'd be happy to," Ethan said firmly, excited about the assignment. "Is there anything else I can do?"

"Just keep doing what you do. I know you'll see that everything's under control."

"Yes, sir, I will."

"I'll see that the meals get on and the house is kept tidy," Mona offered eagerly. "That's what I do."

"Thank you, Mona. We're grateful you're here, for many reasons."

Jon turned to leave, saying, "Ethan, it would also be good if you could bring my meals upstairs since I want to stay close to Maddie and I'm pretty slow."

"Not a problem," Ethan said.

"And I'll send up some broth for Mrs. Brandt," Mona offered.

"Thank you," Jon said, and he left the room.

Throughout lunch it was obvious that Lizzy and Hansen were feeling down; they were concerned about their mother. Since Sara remained mostly quiet, Ethan ventured to play a guessing game with the children that soon distracted them with laughter. He had them help clear the table when lunch was finished, then he started them each drawing a picture to cheer up Maddie. Sara observed for a few minutes, saying nothing until she announced, "I'll be in the parlor," and left the room.

He could hear the piano from the parlor, and he loved the way her music filled the house. He'd never been in a home with a piano before, and he found the effect of one almost magical. He'd heard Maddie play a little here and there, but she was usually busy with other things when he was around.

When the children had finished their pictures, Lizzy said, "We need to do our school lessons. Will you help us, Ethan?" Before he could answer she ran to get a small stack of books from a cupboard and brought them back to the table. He knew that Lizzy wouldn't start going to school in town until next year, but Maddie taught both her children some every day. He was only slightly embarrassed to admit his inability to help. "I'm afraid I can't help you with that, Lizzy. You see, I didn't get much schooling myself, so I wouldn't be able to help you."

"Oh, I remember now," she said as if it were nothing. But Ethan's embarrassment deepened when he looked up to see Sara in the doorway, looking at him as if he'd broken out with purple spots. Only then did he realize the music had stopped a few minutes earlier.

"I'll help you," Sara said to the children, and he wondered if he heard something condescending in her voice, or if it was simply his imagination. He watched her sit down at the table with the children. He wanted to just sit there with them and look at her, but he also wanted to leave, to avoid her disconcerting presence. He wondered what it was that made this woman so attractive when he hardly knew her, and wasn't likely to ever know her any better. In spite of a general condescending air about her, he caught an occasional glance that made him wonder if there was more to her than he could see on the surface.

"I'll be outside," he said. "Ring the bell when you're done, or if you need me."

Ethan unintentionally slammed the door, then he paced back and forth in the barn, as if he could work her out of his head by working out his nervous energy. He finally forced himself to sit on a bale of hay and calm down. A few minutes later he heard the triangle and hurried into the house. He was barely inside the door when Sara said sharply, "I don't feel well. And the children are too worked up from your games to pay attention. I'm going to lie down. Would you please see to the children?"

"I'd be happy to," he said, but knowing that this time he hadn't imagined the condescension in her tone. She made it clear that she considered him only worthy of criticism and command.

"Come on, kids," he said, doing his best to ignore her—and the way she made him feel. "Put your coats on. Let's go outside and—"

"I think it's best if Phillip stays in the house," Sara said, even though the children had already run to get their coats.

"It's a fine day out, Mrs. Hartford," he said, failing at his effort to sound polite. "The children would do well to run and play—wear themselves out a bit. Your brother put me in charge of the children. Why don't you take it up with him, and then you can take a nap."

Sara stood and watched Ethan herd the children out the door. She was too stunned to respond, and too angry to let it go. She hurried upstairs to Jon and Maddie's room, peering in to see Maddie resting and Jon sitting beside the bed, reading. He looked up and saw her, and she whispered, "May I talk to you for a moment?"

Jon took up his crutches and came quietly into the hall, closing the door behind him. "What is it?" he asked. "You look upset."

"Where did you find such a difficult man?" she asked crisply.

Jon laughed. "What? Ethan? He found us, actually. But I've never once seen him behave in a way that was the slightest bit difficult. Well, he did want to eat my piece of pie when I told him he had to pick you up at the station."

Sara scowled at him, and he added playfully, "What did he do that's so difficult?"

"He took the children out to play when I told him I didn't want Phillip going out."

"Is there a reason you didn't want Phillip going out?" he asked. When she hesitated, he added, "I'm certain if you gave Ethan a good reason, he would have agreed."

"Never mind," Sara said. "I'm sorry I bothered you."

She moved away but he grabbed her hand. "What's going on, Sara? You've been awfully tense since you got here; I'll admit that some times are worse than others."

She interrupted angrily, "My husband was killed last month. I've felt sick twenty-four hours a day for nearly eight months. And I'm not in the mood to share my parenting responsibilities with some backward oaf."

Jon's face tightened and his eyes bored into her. "I can't believe you just said that. No matter what might be going on in your life, you cannot come into my home and assume you understand what's going on around here without bothering to ask. Your pain, or your prejudice, will *never* make Ethan Caldwell anything less than one of the most decent, good-hearted, loving people I've ever known. And you will treat him with the same respect that he treats you."

"That shouldn't be too hard," she said, if only to have the last word. But by the time she got to her room, having to go down one staircase and then back up another, she had to admit that the problem was her own. She barely knew Ethan Caldwell, but it wasn't difficult to see that Jon was right. She'd seen no evidence that he wasn't decent and good-hearted. But then why did she feel so uncomfortable around him? Was it simply because she'd never met anyone like him before? Was the problem simply prejudice on her part? Or was it something more? Something deeper? The very idea was unnerving, and she forced it away in order to get her much needed rest.

Sara awoke to a light knock at the door. "Come in," she called, certain it would be Mona.

But she sat up as abruptly as she could manage when Ethan's voice said, "Beg your pardon, ma'am, but you were still sleeping during supper time. Mona just asked me if I'd bring this up for you. She's afraid the journey wore you out."

"Thank you, Mr. Caldwell," she said, wishing it hadn't sounded so terse. He just seemed to bring out the worst in her.

He set the tray on the table near the window. "Will there be anything else, ma'am?" he asked, and she wondered if the subtle ring of sarcasm she detected was just her tense nerves. Or *was* he somehow mocking her?

"Yes, actually," she said. "I wonder if you could tell me how a grown man would be incapable of helping a child with her school lessons."

He looked directly at her with hard eyes, saying, "There are times, Mrs. Hartford, when you are an extremely unkind woman."

Sara was so startled that she couldn't come up with a response, and when she did, the words that came to her mind would only have proved him right. She was grateful that he turned from the room before he could see the tears forming in her eyes, verifying that she agreed with what he'd said. She *was* a very unkind woman. Was that what she'd come all the way out west to discover? That she was unkind? Was that the real woman at her core self?

In spite of diminished appetite, Sara ate the meal Mona had sent, knowing she'd feel terribly ill if she didn't. The nausea had relentlessly persisted with this pregnancy, so unexpected after the last one. But far worse churned the thoughts in her mind, and she was relieved when Jon came to check on her.

"Hello," she said, then returned her gaze to the window, although seeing nothing. Her thoughts were racing so fast she couldn't find one to hold onto and make sense of.

"I'm sorry if I said something earlier to upset you," he said, "but—"

"It's all right," she said. "You told me what I needed to hear, I think."

Following a full minute of silence, he asked, "Where are you?"

"Lost," she said. He sat down nearby, but she remained as she was.

"Do you want to tell me about it, or—"

"Ethan just told me that I am an extremely unkind woman."

Jon chuckled, and she glared at him. "Did he now?" he asked, the mirth evident in his eyes.

"Yes, he did," she said as she stood.

"So, what do you want me to do, Sara? Flog him? Fire him?"

"Don't be ridiculous," she countered, frustrated with his teasing.

His voice softened with gravity. "You can't ridicule a man for being honest."

Her temptation to get defensive was overpowered by her growing desire to see herself realistically. "So, what are you saying, Jon?" she asked quietly. "That he's right?"

"I don't know, Sara. You tell me. Do you think you're unkind?"

Sara sighed and slumped into an overstuffed chair. "Sometimes."

"Yes, well, I'd agree with that. And don't get all upset," he hurried on as he saw her bristling. "You told me you were trying to find yourself. Well, in order to do that, first you're going to have to be honest with yourself. And sometimes it takes someone who cares enough to be honest to help you see what you're so used to that you *don't* see it."

"I think that actually makes sense." She surrendered. "You sound as if you're speaking from experience."

"Oh, yes," he said. "There was a time when I was the only one who couldn't see that I was meant to be a doctor, and that I was good at it. I had to get pretty down and dirty with myself before I could lower my pride enough to see that they were right."

"All right, Jon, I'm doing my best to lower my pride. So, why don't you tell me what you think of me?"

"You're not going to hurt me, are you?"

"No," she laughed softly and tried to relax, "I'm not going to hurt you. Please, just talk to me."

"All right. I think you're a good woman with a good heart. I also think you get so caught up in the little world surrounding you that you don't stop to consider how the rest of the world might appear to other people. You have a way of being . . . dare I say, condescending? You believe things should be a certain way, and when they're not, you're not very tolerant."

Sara allowed that to sink in for a few moments, and Jon allowed her enough silence to do so. It only took her a second to get past the temptation to be angry at his accusations, and to realize that he was right. Then a thought occurred to her and she blurted out, "You just described our father."

He smiled widely. "Imagine that," he said with mild sarcasm.

"Good heavens," she said, feeling her heart quicken with the realization. "I used to get so annoyed with that condescending attitude of his. And now I'm . . . Oh Jon. I don't want to be that way. Tell me what to do."

Jon leaned forward, putting his forearms on his thighs. "I don't have all the answers, Sara. And I think we just have to come to terms with who and what we are one step at a time, but . . . well . . . I believe it's a good thing to try and understand what life might be like for other people. We've been very blessed, Sara. We have no idea what it's like to go hungry, or to wonder how we're going to feed our children. Or what it's like not having the opportunity for an education." She felt her back stiffen, almost wondering if he'd overheard her conversation with Ethan. But the comment seemed completely innocent.

"I think," he went on, "when you meet someone, you ought to just try and imagine what their life might have been like. I gained a deeper love and respect for our father by learning of his struggles. And the same for Maddie's father. I don't know if that's the answer, Sara. But it might give you something to think about."

Sara nodded, certain he was right. "How is Maddie?" she asked.

"The fever was low and it's gone now. She's got a good appetite. I think it was just a bug. But I want her to stay down. She's got all the signs of being ready for labor."

"You'll let me know when the pains start? Even if it's the middle of the night?"

"You need your rest as well, sweet sister."

"I was with her when Lizzy was born. I want to be with her now. She'll be able to return the favor in not so many weeks."

Jon smiled. "I'll let you know," he said, and hobbled out of the room.

Sara returned her gaze to the window. She suddenly had an urge to talk to Ethan Caldwell.

CHAPTER 4
Something In Common

Sara prayed she wouldn't make a fool of herself as she stepped into the barn to find Ethan. He was there, pitching hay to the horses by the light of a single lantern. He glanced toward her briefly. It was evident he was surprised to see her there, but he said nothing.

"Hello," she said.

"Hello," he repeated and continued his work.

"There's something I need to say to you."

"I'm listening," he said.

"You are right, Mr. Caldwell. Sometimes I *am* very unkind. But I don't want to be." She took a deep breath and acted on her impulse to confide in him. "I sold everything I had and came out here because I wanted to find myself . . . I wanted to discover who I am. Some of what I'm discovering isn't very pleasant, but I want to change. I want to be . . . kinder, and . . . I just wanted to say that I appreciate your honesty, and, well, your courage. And I was hoping . . . maybe you could help me out a little. I mean, I admit that my life has been very secluded, and I'd like to know what your life has been like. In truth, what I asked you earlier was out of genuine curiosity, Mr. Caldwell." She laughed uncomfortably and glanced down to notice she had been wringing her hands. "I must confess I've never known anyone like you."

"Well, that gives us something in common," he said, more sarcastic than humorous.

She let it go and continued, "So, I want to apologize for the way I sounded upstairs, and . . . would you let me try again." She cleared her throat carefully and looked directly at him. "Having been as blessed as I've been, I can't help wondering what kind of circumstances would leave you with so little opportunity for an education."

Sara held her breath, fearing that, even with this approach, he would be offended by the question. He stuck the pitchfork into the hay and left it there. He put his hands on his hips and stated, "It happens when staying fed takes priority over being able to read and write. If I hadn't gone to work we would have starved. Simple as that."

Sara allowed his statement to settle; she felt somehow horrified by the very idea of a child working to survive. Without even trying, her heart filled with compassion, and she suddenly believed she wasn't beyond redemption. She wanted to tell him she was sorry, but she felt certain pity wasn't something he'd receive well. Instead she ventured to offer, "I would consider it a privilege to be able to help you learn what you haven't had the opportunity to learn—only if you want to, of course."

Again he looked at her long and hard, as if he were trying to figure something out. Finally he said, "I'll think about it. Thank you for the offer. And for the apology."

Sara suddenly felt emotional and exhausted. Fearing she'd either burst into tears or pass out, she simply nodded and left the barn, wishing deep inside that he would accept her offer. She felt a growing desire to be close to Ethan Caldwell, although she didn't try to figure out why.

Sara slept well that night—the exhaustion of pregnancy outweighing the effects of numerous thoughts tumbling through her mind. She woke up and immediately thought of Ethan. But instead of feeling disconcerted, she smiled and got dressed, pleased with the prospect of seeing him at breakfast. She barely had her shoes on when Jon knocked at the door.

"Come in," she called.

He opened the door and said, "Maddie's pains started a while ago. She's asking for you. If you'll sit with her, I'll have Mona send up some breakfast. I have a couple of appointments this morning, but it shouldn't take long."

"Of course," Sara said, and hurried to Maddie's room. She didn't stop to see anyone but Phillip on the way.

"How are you doing?" she asked, taking a moment to hug him tightly.

"I like it here," he said with a little smile. "I'm glad we're going to live here now."

"So am I," she said. "Listen, I think Aunt Maddie's going to have her baby today, and I'm going to go sit with her and help her. I want you to stay with Hansen and Lizzy and be a good boy, just the way you have been."

He nodded firmly and broke into a grin. "Ethan said it would probably snow today, and he said we could make a snowman and have a snowball fight."

"That sounds exciting," she said and he hurried away to find his cousins.

Sara sighed and moved on toward Maddie's room, wondering if Ethan Caldwell had any idea how much he'd already made up for five years of Harrison's poor fathering.

Sara found Maddie calmly enduring pains of three minutes apart. She was not terribly uncomfortable and seemed in good spirits. They reminisced about when Lizzy had been born in Boston, and Sara admitted, "You know, Maddie, I must confess that your stay in Boston is one of the highlights of my life. You helped me through the transition of losing my father more than you'll ever know. You're the sister I never had, and I'm so grateful for the chance to grow old here, right along with you."

Maddie got tears in her eyes and squeezed Sara's hand. "The feeling is mutual, Sara. I'm so grateful to have you here with me now." She endured a sharp pain, then laughed softly. "And now we'll have another set of cousins who will be the best of friends." Maddie's eyes turned sorrowful as she said, "I haven't had the chance to tell you how very sorry I am for your loss. I simply can't imagine losing a husband. I don't think I could bear it if I were to lose Jon."

Sara looked down, feeling the guilt creep into her heart. She recalled Jon saying that if she were going to find herself, she had to first be honest with herself—and with those she loved, she concluded. She readily admitted to her thoughts, "It's been difficult, Maddie, but not for the reasons you might think."

Maddie endured another pain, then asked, "What do you mean?"

Sara smiled and squeezed her hand. "Now is not the time. But after this baby gets here, and you're feeling better, we'll have a real heart-to-heart talk. I promise."

Maddie nodded, and a moment later a light knock sounded at the door. "Come in," Sara called, and Ethan stepped into the room with a tray.

"Mona sent breakfast up for you, Mrs. Hartford, but the doctor said that Mrs. Brandt shouldn't eat."

Sara stood up. "I'll go eat in the next room Maddie, so you won't—"

"No, it's fine," Maddie said. "I want you to be with me. I'm not even hungry. It won't bother me."

Ethan set the tray on the dresser and Sara said appreciatively, "Thank you, Ethan."

He smiled and moved toward the door, seeming extremely nervous.

"Ethan?" Maddie said, and reached a hand toward him.

"Yes, ma'am," he said, and took it with little hesitation.

"You be sure and make yourself at home, even though I'm not keeping track of you for a few days. Promise?"

"Yes, ma'am," he said again just as another contraction came on. Maddie groaned and took her breath in short spurts. Sara could see that it was getting worse. She almost forgot about Ethan's presence until he spoke in an agitated voice, "What's wrong with her? Why is she . . . hurting like that? Don't let—"

"Ethan." Sara stood and looked into his eyes. "She's going to be fine." He glanced past her to Maddie, apparently unconvinced. "The pain is a normal part of having a baby. She's going to be just fine."

"How do you know?" he asked. The question was without accusation, only an innocent concern.

"I worked for many years assisting my father. He was one of Boston's finest physicians." She saw the surprise, and perhaps even some comfort, in his eyes. "I've helped deliver many, many babies, Ethan," she continued. "The pain is normal. She's going to be fine. Now, you go and see to the children. Jon will be back here soon, and we'll both take very good care of her."

Ethan nodded firmly. He glanced once more toward Maddie, who was relaxing now, then he quickly left the room. Sara wondered why he would be so concerned. She knew he had grown to care for Jon and Maddie, but his worry seemed almost unnatural given the circumstances.

Feeling a little queasy as she often did, Sara hurried to eat her breakfast. She knew she needed her strength to help Maddie through the day. Maddie's previous labors had been long with both Lizzy and Hansen, and Sara suspected it would be many hours before this was over.

* * * * *

Ethan was grateful for the distraction of watching the children. He struggled to tear his thoughts from what Maddie might be going through upstairs. He hated the memories he associated with child-bearing, and found himself often glancing to the spot on the kitchen floor where Hannah had died in his arms.

"Why don't we all put on our coats and go out to the barn for a while," he suggested.

"Can we play in the snow?" Phillip asked. His expression was so eager that Ethan wondered if they had snow in Boston.

"Haven't you ever seen snow before?" Ethan asked him.

"Well, sure, but my papa never let me go play in it."

Ethan chuckled, but wondered what kind of man this Harrison Hartford had been. He wondered more prominently what kind of life Sara and her son had been living, and he felt sorry for them.

"The thing is," Ethan said, "it's just starting to snow now, and if we go out and play in it, we'll get nothing but wet. If we wait until there's lots of it on the ground, then we can have some real fun."

Phillip nodded in acceptance of the explanation, then they all went to the barn and Ethan let them play in the loft while he sat at the edge to make sure none of them got too close. He couldn't help laughing at their antics and their vivid imaginations. But his mind was still absorbed with Maddie Brandt. He prayed silently, over and over, that she would be all right. Then he thought of Sara having to go through it in a matter of weeks and he groaned aloud.

"Is something wrong, Ethan?" Lizzy asked.

"No, pumpkin, but I think it's about time for lunch. Five more minutes and we need to go in." They all protested, but ten minutes later the triangle rang and they reluctantly went inside. Sara was seated at the table, looking tired and drawn. But she smiled when Phillip hugged her and told her what they'd been doing. While Phillip was washing up with his cousins, Ethan had to ask her, "Is Mrs. Brandt . . ."

"She's fine," Sara said. "Jon is with her. It's progressing normally."

Ethan nodded and went to wash up as well. "It sure does smell good, Mona," he said to her.

"I hope it tastes good too," Mona said with a little laugh.

"I'm not worried about that," he said. "It's a good thing we don't have to rely on my cooking while Mrs. Brandt is laid up."

"Well, I'm glad to be here," Mona said as they all gathered at the table.

The children chattered amongst themselves, still carrying on with the game they'd been playing in the loft. Apparently Lizzy was the queen, and Hansen and Phillip were great knights that she would send to hunt for an evil dragon.

Ethan's attention was drawn from the children's conversation when Mona said, "I sure can't help thinking about when Jon and Maddie came to Boston, and little Lizzy was born."

"I've been thinking about that too," Sara said. "So much has changed since then, and yet it wasn't so many years ago." Ethan saw her eyes become sad and distant as she said, "I remember when I had Phillip . . . I desperately longed for Maddie to be there with me. But Harrison . . ." She stopped and glanced at Ethan as if she'd just recalled that he was there. He watched as huge tears rose in her eyes.

"Forgive me," Sara said, and hurried from the table.

The children were apparently too caught up in their game to notice. Mona appeared concerned, but she said nothing. Ethan quickly finished his meal, then acted on his instincts, hoping they would not see him a fool. He found Sara sitting on a sofa in the parlor, gazing toward the window. He stood in the doorway and said quietly, "Forgive me, ma'am, for intruding on your privacy, but . . . I just wanted to say that . . . I know how hard it is to lose someone you've shared your life with, and well, it's been my experience that talking to someone who knows how you feel can be mighty helpful."

She looked at him long and hard, but said nothing. Ethan wished he'd just kept to himself and hurried to say, "It was just an offer." He turned to walk away. "You know where to find me if—"

"No, wait," she said, and he turned back. "Please, sit down." She slid over on the sofa to make room for him.

Ethan took a deep breath and sat next to her, fidgeting with his hands.

"How did you come to terms with losing someone that . . . you shared your life with?" she asked.

Ethan chuckled self-consciously. "Well, I didn't come to terms with it very well at all . . . until recently. I guess you could say my experience is the bad example that you wouldn't want to follow. I took to drinking, just like my papa did when we lost my mama. It took me a lot of years to come to my senses, and I never would have been able to do that without a lot of help from the good Lord above. It was when I started praying again that I found what I needed inside me to keep going, to quit drinking, and find peace. So, I guess it's the praying that made the difference. I don't know how we could ever get through much of anything without knowing that we're not alone."

Sara looked at him with warmth in her eyes, though it didn't quite disguise her doubt. He wondered what she might be doubting. He wondered what he could say or do to help her ease those doubts. But mostly, he wondered why he had to feel so concerned about her at all. He was searching for words to break the silence when they heard Jon's urgent call from upstairs, "Sara. I need you."

"Oh my," she said and hurried away. Ethan's concern over how Sara perceived his words quickly vanished beneath his fear for Maddie.

Ethan nearly went mad through the afternoon, trapped in the house while snow continued to fall outside. The children were quietly occupied up in Phillip's room. Ethan sat in the relative silence and concluded his distance was a good thing when he could hear an occasional cry of pain from Maddie's room. He went upstairs every little while to check on the children, only to find them still caught up in their game of queens, knights, and dragons.

"Thank you, Lord," he murmured for the tenth time that hour, grateful that they were not antsy and wanting him to play with them. He felt as tight as a bowstring. He went out to the barn half a dozen times, only to find that there was nothing to do. He paced the porch. He paced the parlor. He avoided the kitchen where Mona kept busy making bread and pies and some chicken concoction that she declared he'd love.

A short while before supper time, Sara finally came down the stairs. Ethan didn't want to make a fool of himself, but he couldn't keep from blurting, "Is she all right? Is she—"

"She's fine, Ethan," Sara said with a warm smile. "It's a girl. And everything's fine."

"Oh," he said. Then he laughed and noticed he actually had tears in his eyes. Without thinking about it first, he quickly embraced Sara.

She laughed with him, then their eyes met and his concern for Maddie was quickly replaced by his fears for where this feeling might lead him. To no good, he felt certain, and forced his attention elsewhere.

Ethan rode out to let Maddie's parents know about the baby, as well as Jon's aunt and uncle, Ellie and Dave. They were all thrilled with the news, but both households had been fighting coughs and sniffles with the oncoming season, and they didn't want to get the baby sick. They sent word back with him that they'd be over to visit when they got feeling better.

The children buzzed excitedly at supper over the new baby. The chicken dish Mona had made prompted Ethan's compliments, "You were right, Mona. This is great. What is it, anyway?"

"It's called chicken cordon blue."

"It must be a Boston thing," he said.

"Actually, it's French," she told him quite seriously. Whatever it was, Ethan really liked it.

Sara ate, and then went upstairs to be with Maddie while Jon came down and ate. He told the children they could see the baby in the morning. When they were finished eating, they had a brief scripture study and prayer, while Sara remained upstairs with Maddie. Jon relieved Ethan of his childcare duties and took the children upstairs to personally see them to bed.

Ethan sat alone in the parlor, wondering why he felt so exhausted when he'd hardly done anything all day. His relief over Maddie's well being was indescribable, but familiar ironies began to haunt him, and he had to force himself to count his blessings instead. He told himself he should go check on the animals and get to bed, but for the moment he was content to just sit and let the day catch up with him.

* * * * *

Sara sat in the rocker near Maddie's bed, holding the new baby close. While Maddie slept, Sara let her emotions free. The miracle of birth, combined with the heartache of all she'd been through, caused the tears to flow steadily down her face. She was startled to hear Jon ask, "What's wrong, Sara?"

"Oh," she said, wiping at her tears while she looked at the baby sleeping against her arm, "just a little of everything, I suppose."

"Hmm. I'm surprised that I haven't seen you crying a whole lot more then." He sat down and set his crutches aside. "I can't imagine going through what you've been through. If I were to lose Maddie . . ." He gazed lovingly at his wife, and Sara wondered how it might feel to have a man care that much about her. She needed to tell Jon the truth, that her grief was more for the unhappiness of her life, than for the loss of a husband who turned out to be nothing she'd hoped for. But now wasn't the time. They were all tired and she didn't want to mar this day for him.

In a way that had become almost familiar, Sara's mind drifted to Ethan Caldwell. She thought of his earlier reaction to Maddie's pain, and the emotion she'd seen in his eyes when she'd told him that it was over and everything was all right. Just recalling his panic chilled her, and she felt prompted to share her thoughts with Jon. "Ethan was terribly concerned about Maddie. I wonder why it would be so hard for him, when he's not known either of you for very long."

Jon looked at Sara with a gaze that was almost as chilling as Ethan's had been. "Ethan once owned this house," he said, and Sara's eyes widened in surprise. "Of course it was much smaller then, and when we bought it, it'd been empty for a few years. Apparently, after Ethan lost his wife, he started drinking. He lost his job, then his house. He's been living with an uncle, I believe, somewhere in the valley. He finally quit drinking, started going to church, and came to terms with the loss. But I know it's been hard for him. It's probably been about ten years."

Sara appreciated learning a little more of Ethan's background, but it didn't tell her what she wanted to know. "That's all nice to know, Jon, but you didn't answer my question."

He looked briefly unsure, then his eyes softened in compassion. "From what he told us, she was pregnant, but not full term. He said she was standing by the stove one minute, and curled up on the floor in pain the next. Apparently she hemorrhaged; bled to death in his arms, right there on the kitchen floor."

Sara moaned and put a hand over her mouth. Fresh tears pressed beneath her closed eyelids. She swallowed carefully and said, "I can't even imagine . . . how horrible such an experience would be."

"Neither can I," Jon said, gazing again at Maddie. His voice softened further as he went on, "The ironic thing is that he'd wished with everything he had that there could have been a doctor here, and now . . . a doctor lives here." He turned to look at Sara and said firmly, "I probably could have saved her life, Sara. If I had been here, she might still be here. He could have had a beautiful family by now. I know we can't question why life turns out the way it does, and I know we have to make the most of what we've been given. But . . . it's difficult to think of what he's suffered. Still, it's taken him some time, but he's a good example of enduring. He has almost nothing to his name, but he's happy and full of gratitude for what little he does have. He's a good man—completely without guile. And I pray every day that he can find someone to bring back the happiness he's lost."

Sara became a little preoccupied with the heartache she was feeling on Ethan's behalf, and Jon almost startled her when he said, "You must be exhausted. I'm going to get some rest while the baby sleeps. You need to get your rest too. I'll see you in the morning."

Sara set the baby into the cradle near the bed. She kissed her brother's cheek, squeezed his hand, and went slowly down the stairs. She noticed a lamp on in the parlor and thought she should turn it out, since Jon wouldn't be coming back down. But she entered to find Ethan sitting on the sofa, obviously in a stupor of thought as well. All she'd learned of him today made her realize that she was getting in touch with herself. The compassion she felt for him evoked other deep emotions, and she felt herself opening up. Something she hadn't allowed in years—or ever, perhaps.

He looked up and she said, "Forgive me for disturbing you. I saw the lamp on and didn't want to leave it burning, but obviously you'll take care of it before you leave and . . . well, good night."

"You didn't disturb me," Ethan said. Sara smiled, but she felt torn between wanting to be with him and feeling she should leave. "You doing all right?" he asked.

"I'm tired, but it's been a good day. There's nothing like a new baby to put life in perspective." He glanced down abruptly, and she quickly added, "I'm sorry. I didn't mean to be insensitive." He looked surprised. "Jon told me about the way you lost your wife . . . and baby. I just want to say how sorry I am and . . . May I sit down?"

"Of course," he said, and she sat beside him on the sofa, just as he had done earlier when consoling her.

"I just wanted to say that . . . first of all, I appreciate your concern for me this afternoon. We were interrupted then, but I must confess that I was intrigued by the way you said how hard it is to lose someone you've shared your life with. You see, Mr. Caldwell, I—"

"Please," he said, "call me Ethan. I don't do well with formalities and such."

"Very well, Ethan. As I was saying, I shared a great deal of my life with Harrison, but the truth is . . ." She hesitated as the words formed in her mouth.

"You all right?" he asked sensitively. She was touched by his reaction to her emotions. She recalled crying openly in front of Harrison, and receiving no acknowledgment to her emotion whatsoever.

"I'm fine," she said. "Thank you for asking." Then she sighed. "I've never admitted this aloud to anyone before, not anyone. For some reason, you're just easy to talk to. Maybe it's because, as you said, you've lost someone and . . . Well, the point is, I never really loved him. I know that now." She was amazed at how good it felt to openly acknowledge the truth. "We were fond of each other . . . at one time, but . . . there were aspects of our relationship that quickly squelched what good we had shared. It seemed that once we had been married a matter of weeks, everything that had seemed so right had all gone wrong."

Sara took a deep breath and looked directly at him. "So, I can't say that I understand your grief, Ethan, because I've come to see that the grief I feel is more for the life I never got to share. And I feel guilty when I realize that I didn't grieve at all for my husband's death. I see it as a blessing—I feel free."

He gave her a searching gaze. "Don't you ever feel lonely?" he asked.

"Yes, but . . . it's better to be by yourself and a little lonely than to be living under the same roof with someone and feeling completely alone. At least now there's a tangible reason for being lonely. However, I'm here with family now, so I'm certain that everything will be better."

"I hope so, ma'am. You deserve to be happy."

"Thank you, Ethan. You're very sweet. And you deserve to be happy, too."

"Oh, I am," he said so genuinely that she felt encouraged even further. "Just lonely," he added, shrugging his shoulders as if it were a minor inconvenience. Yet she could see the truth in his eyes. His loneliness tormented him, and her heart ached on his behalf.

"You should be getting to bed, Mrs. Hartford," he said as he rose. "You've got to take care of yourself . . . and that baby."

"Yes, I know you're right," she said, coming to her feet. "And please . . . call me Sara."

He looked surprised, but he smiled widely. "Very well, Sara. May I walk you to your room, just to make sure you get there all right?"

Sara didn't foresee any difficulty in getting to her room, but she readily accepted, "Thank you. I'd appreciate that."

Ethan took the lamp into one hand and motioned for her to go ahead of him into the hall. They said nothing as they went slowly up the back stairs and stopped at the door of her room. He handed the lamp to her and said, "I can make my way back just fine. Good night. Sleep well."

"Good night, Ethan. And thank you."

He nodded and disappeared into the dark hall. She heard his footsteps on the stairs, then the back door open and close again. She sighed, quickly undressed for bed, and climbed between the covers, unable to recall when she had felt so secure and at peace. She recalled what Ethan had said about prayer getting him through. She'd never practiced prayer as a personal habit, but she thought it might be a good thing to take up. She looked up through the darkness and said softly, "Thank you, God, for bringing me here safely, for giving me a good brother and his sweet family, and for the safe arrival of the new baby. And thank you for giving me a new friend. Guide me, please. Help me find peace. Amen."

She sighed with contentment. She liked the way it felt to talk to God. Feeling somehow confident that her prayer would be heard, she drifted into a deep, peaceful slumber.

* * * * *

For more than two weeks Ethan did his best to stay busy—as far away from Sara Hartford as he could manage. They saw each other at meals, and exchanged amiable greetings in passing. But it seemed that caution was required with such strong, and unexplainable, emotions. Maddie recovered quickly from her childbirth, and many visitors came with gifts, including Maddie's parents and Dave and Ellie. In fact, the four spent a great deal of time at the house, cooing over the baby and enjoying each other's company. They were always big-hearted with Ethan, encouraging him to be involved. But having Sara there made him somehow reluctant. He couldn't put a finger on the reasons. He just found being with her unsettling, in spite of the warm conversations they'd shared.

Since Jon wanted to keep an eye on Maddie, Ethan took the children to church the first Sunday after the baby was born. He loved being at church for a number of reasons. While there had been a few people who seemed inclined to retain previous judgments, most were gracious and warm, and their kindness helped him feel more accepted. Ethan also liked wearing the clothes that Jon had given him. He discovered his build wasn't exactly like Jon's, since the pants were just a bit too short, as were the sleeves of the shirt and coat, and the shoes were just a little too big, though they could be managed with an extra pair of socks. But beyond that they fit him rather well, and Maddie had graciously redone the hems so the pants and coat fit perfectly. He almost felt like a gentleman wearing such fine clothes. He figured when he had enough money saved up, he was going to buy some nicer clothes that fit better. But he wanted to have plenty of money first, so the clothes wouldn't take all he had.

The following Sunday, Jon went with Ethan and the children. Sara had talked about wanting to go the previous evening, but she ended up not feeling well and declined. Ethan was decidedly relieved, but felt guilty for such thoughts when getting her out to church could have been such a good thing. That evening, during scripture study time, Ethan could hardly keep his eyes off Sara. The increased time she'd been there had not lessened his fascination with her. If anything, it had only grown stronger. She had proven to be a fine woman in all respects, as far as he could see. He just wished he didn't have to be *so* intrigued with her.

After prayer the children started asking questions about Christmas, and they ended up having a lengthy discussion on the family's plans for the holiday. Ethan tried to get up and leave, but Jon said firmly, "We're not going to let you leave here before Christmas, Ethan. You've got to stay into the new year, at least. So, you might as well be in on the plans."

"Well, that would be nice," he said, "but I don't know if—"

"Now, you know I'm not going to be up and around before then," Jon said. "I should have this wretched splint off, but it will take some time to get this foot working again. And where would you go for the holidays if you weren't here?"

"That's a good question," Ethan admitted, glancing at Sara. He hated the idea that he had absolutely nothing to call his own, and nowhere to call home beyond the generosity of these good people. He listened while they discussed plans for their Christmas celebrations, even though it was barely past Thanksgiving. While the idea of being with this family forever appealed to him, more than he dared admit, he knew it simply wasn't meant to be. He had to remember that it was only temporary.

* * * * *

Ethan knelt by the bed to say his prayer as usual, but his mind was so focused on Sara Hartford that he couldn't even find the words to begin. When several minutes of effort proved futile, he finally said, "Please God, just get her out of my head. She's very pretty, and she's actually turned out to be a lot kinder than I thought she would be. But I know that setting my sights on her is about as silly as a horse thinking it can fly. I'm grateful to be here and to be needed by these folks, but once Jon's foot heals up I'll need to be moving on, and I don't need this woman in my head making what's hard for me even harder. I'm trying to be grateful for all You've given me, and I am. I'm grateful, Lord. But it's mighty lonely without Hannah. I'd like to find me another wife someday and have a go at it again. But this just isn't possible. I know it. So, please, just get her out of my head. Let me be her friend if she needs me, but let me be free of these thoughts and feelings—they'll bring me to nothing good. Please, God. Are You hearing me? I know I'm just a poor boy with not much to speak of, but then, so was Joseph Smith, and You know how I feel about him.

And I know how You feel about him. And I know You've answered my prayers before. I know You've guided me and given me strength and peace. And now I'm asking You to just get her out of my head. Please, God. I just need to get some sleep and . . ."

Ethan stopped abruptly as something warm began to fill him. He recognized the feeling, and he squeezed his eyes closed, hoping to hold it close. The Spirit had guided him little by little along the steps to reclaiming his life. And he felt some relief now to know that his prayers were being heard, and he would soon be free of Sara Hartford. His past experiences with the Spirit had always been subtle and fleeting, but undeniable nevertheless. The warmth began to grow until it gradually consumed him. He felt tears burning down his cheeks while he marveled at his blessings. He'd heard talk of such powerful experiences, but he'd never believed he could be worthy of such a grand manifestation of God's existence. And then Ethan felt the thoughts in his head shift dramatically. Instantly, an entire spectrum of understanding opened in his mind. He gasped and opened his eyes, as if grasping the reality of his surroundings could make him accept what he'd just learned. But looking around him didn't change what he knew. And that warm feeling continued to hover until he finally had to admit that his prayer had been answered. Even though the answer was something he'd neither expected nor wanted.

"Good heavens," he muttered, and sat hard on the floor, drained of all strength. The tangible warmth filtered away just as it had come, but the words remained plainly in his mind, as if God himself had spoken them. *Keep her in your heart, Ethan. She belongs in your thoughts.* He gasped again, and then he groaned at the reality before him. He wondered if Moses had felt like this when the Lord told him he had to free the people of Israel. Ethan had gotten on his knees wanting only to get Sara Hartford out of his head. He came unsteadily to his feet, feelings for her penetrating every corner of his soul. He felt alarmingly terrified and amazingly comforted at the same time. He knew somehow that everything would be all right—eventually. It was the getting there that concerned him, and he crawled into bed admonishing himself to be careful about what he prayed for.

* * * * *

Sara fell asleep with Ethan Caldwell on her mind, just as he had been the past couple of weeks. She woke up the same way. While she'd fought to keep him out of her thoughts, this morning she indulged in pondering over what her interest might mean. Without coming to any firm conclusions, she hurried to get dressed and go down to breakfast. It was difficult to tell if she was motivated by her need to have something in her stomach, or her desire to see Ethan. She stopped just short of going out the bedroom door when she heard a rhythmic noise outside. Turning to the window, she could see Ethan down in the yard, chopping wood. The day was bright and there were several inches of new snow on the ground. But Ethan was without a coat while he swung the axe over and over, sending it through one piece of wood after another. She couldn't resist just watching him while she contemplated her feelings. She admitted that she'd never known anyone like Ethan before, but initially she had seen only a backward, uneducated simpleton. She saw more than that now. He was a man, simple as that, but she was intrigued over what kind of a man he was. Her father had certainly been masculine, as was her brother. But they were doctors—their hands were always clean, and their work of a delicate nature. She knew Jon wasn't afraid to work hard outdoors, and she knew that he did, but she'd never actually seen him do it. And Harrison. She made a disgruntled noise at the very idea. Harrison had never lifted anything beyond a pen or a newspaper. In contrast to what she saw before her now, Harrison Hartford had been a milksop.

Oblivious to the passing time, she continued to watch Ethan, easily making out the movement of his muscular shoulders beneath his shirt. She was startled to feel her heart quicken, then felt herself turn warm as she acknowledged what she'd been feeling. *Was it possible?* Yes, she concluded, it certainly was. She had to admit it. She'd become attracted to him. Or perhaps she had been from the very first minute, and she'd simply been reluctant to recognize it for what it was.

Sara was surprised to hear the axe's rhythm stop. She jolted herself from her thoughts to realize that Ethan was looking directly at her. The intensity in his eyes quickened her heart even further, but she wondered why she felt unworthy of her feelings. She was relieved when he turned away, and she watched him go toward the barn. She took a minute to steady her thoughts, then went down to find Mona putting breakfast on the table, and Maddie nursing the baby with a little blanket thrown over her shoulder. As usual, Jon had his foot propped up on a chair, reading a book. The children appeared and they were ready to say the blessing, but Ethan hadn't arrived.

"I rang the triangle," Mona said.

"I believe he's in the barn," Sara said. "Let's go ahead and bless it and I'll go and get him."

Jon gave her a sly smile and she wondered if he sensed what she was feeling. She told herself she should be ashamed for being attracted to a man so soon after her husband's death, then she forced the thought from her mind while Jon prayed over their meal.

Sara slipped into her long coat and trudged through the snow to the barn. She entered to see Ethan pacing frantically back and forth, apparently very upset.

"Is something wrong?" she asked, and closed the door. He almost jumped, then looked at her as if she'd scared him to death.

"No," he said. "I mean . . . I just need to be alone right now. Thank you for asking."

"You're missing breakfast."

"Go ahead and eat. I'll get something later."

Sara almost left, then asked, "Is there something you want to talk about?"

"Uh . . . no . . . thank you, anyway."

Sara nodded and went back to the house, feeling concerned and uneasy. She shook the snow off of her shoes on the back porch, and entered the kitchen as Mona asked, "Is he coming?"

"I don't think so," she said. "He seems terribly upset over something, but he wouldn't tell me what."

A few minutes later, Jon came to his feet with the help of his crutches. "I think I'll go talk to him."

"How can you go out in the snow like that?" Mona demanded.

Jon chuckled and leaned on one crutch, then the other, to put on his coat. "Not to worry, Mona. It's only to the barn. I can assure you I'll return in one piece."

Mona made a disgusted noise, then she laughed softly. Sara

watched her brother leave, wondering how she was ever going to come to terms with her feelings for Ethan.

CHAPTER 5

Fire and Ice

Ethan watched Sara leave and began his pacing again. The hope and comfort he'd felt last night had been replaced by an unfathomable fear. He'd risen earlier than usual with practically no sleep behind him, and got through the regular chores much faster than normal. He'd gone out to chop wood, purposely leaving his coat behind, hoping the hard work and cold air would startle him to his senses. He knew in his heart what he'd felt last night in answer to his prayer. He could never deny it. But logic had quickly marched in to do battle with his feelings. The logic of the situation was . . . well, there wasn't any. No logic whatsoever.

"I've got to be out of my mind," he murmured for the tenth time in as many minutes.

The barn door opened again and he held his breath. If he had to face Sara one more time . . . . Jon appeared, and Ethan breathed a sigh of relief. "Oh, it's you," he said and resumed his pacing.

Jon chuckled and sat on a bale of hay, where he took up brushing the snow from the large sock covering his splinted foot. "What's going on, Ethan?" Jon asked. When he said nothing, Jon persisted. "I have never seen you like this. What's up? Come on, you can tell me."

"Well, I ought to tell somebody, I guess," he said. "But if you want to know the truth, I prefer to keep it to myself. Maybe if I don't tell you, or anybody else, then I'll never have to face it, but . . . Ooh! I keep thinking about that Jonah story."

"Jonah?" Jon chuckled again. "What about him?"

"When he didn't do what the Lord had told him to do, he got swallowed by that stupid fish. Well, I told the Lord if He could help me stop drinking, and keep me fed, I'd do whatever He wanted me to do. Well, now I know what He wants me to do, and a bottle of whiskey sounds mighty pleasant right now."

"Don't you dare!" Jon said vehemently.

"Believe it or not, I *wouldn't* dare," Ethan said, still pacing. "I may be a fool, but I'm not stupid enough to go back to that. I wouldn't. I couldn't."

"Well, I'm glad to hear that, but maybe you'd better tell me what you're so upset about."

"It's that sister of yours. Blast her! I can't believe she'd do this to me."

"What? What has she done?" Jon demanded, as if he might go find her right now and reprimand her.

"She looked at me just right," he said, leaving Jon all the more confused. "And after I told her what I thought of her, she apologized and got all nice on me. I was beginning to think I wouldn't want her even if I *could* have her, and then she had to go soft on me, and she's been so kind and polite—"

"Ethan!" Jon said and then laughed. "You're attracted to my sister?"

Ethan stopped for a moment and glared at him, then started pacing again.

"You are," Jon guessed, and laughed again.

"So, what if I am? What would you expect me to do about it? We're as different as night and day. Winter and summer. Fire and ice." He hit his forehead with both hands. "Listen to me. I can't believe I'm telling you all this. But I've got to tell somebody. I've got to."

"Ethan, sit down. You're making me tired."

Ethan did as he was told, realizing that he was tired as well. "Oh, Jon," he said, pressing his face into his hands. "What am I going to do? I prayed and prayed that God would just get her out of my head."

"Apparently your prayer wasn't answered."

"Oh, it was answered all right. Have you ever had that feeling like . . . like . . . God's putting words right into your head, and you know it's from Him, and your whole body feels like it's on fire?"

"Yes, actually," Jon said, his voice turning grave, "I have."

"Well, that's what happened," Ethan said, pressing his fingers together and leaning his forearms on his thighs. "How can you dispute an answer when it comes like that?"

Jon's seriousness made it clear that he understood and respected such spiritual experiences. He leaned forward and asked seriously, "What was the answer, Ethan?"

Ethan looked into the eyes of his new friend and felt more calm than he had in hours. Forming the words in his mind somehow brought back the tranquility of the initial experience. He closed his eyes as if that might help him savor the peace, knowing it could be a light to guide him through the confusion. He kept his eyes closed, finding it somehow easier when talking about the sensitive subject. "I prayed that she would just leave my head. I was told that she was supposed to be there." He heard Jon gasp but ignored him and went on. "She belongs in my head, my heart, my soul. I'm the one meant to care for her, protect her," his voice cracked, "love her . . . and her children."

"That's incredible," Jon said breathlessly, and Ethan opened his eyes to look at him. He almost expected him to laugh, or mock him, or insist that it was ridiculous. But his expression was so serene and in awe that Ethan had to believe Jon found some measure of truth in what he'd said.

"I can't explain how I know, Jon, but I know. I *know* that the Lord wants me to be with her. But . . . how can that be possible? I can't make her feel something for me if she doesn't feel it. I can't make decisions like that for her. And look at her. She's so fine . . . and so educated . . . such a lady. And look at me. I'm just . . ."

"Ethan," Jon said in a firm, quiet voice that got his attention, "you're a good man. You could be the best thing that ever happened to her. It's true that you can't make decisions for her. She's a free agent. You can only do what's in your power to let her know how you feel, and let time take its course. There's no hurry, Ethan. She just lost her husband. She's going to need some time."

Ethan thought of her confession that she'd never loved her husband, but he didn't figure it was his place to tell Jon about that. He continued with another point. "But . . . how could I ever provide for a woman like that? How could I ever make her happy? What would we talk about for the next fifty years when I can't even read?"

"Ethan," Jon said again, "that's fear talking. It was fear that put Jonah into such a mess. If you know in your heart what the Lord wants you to do, you're going to have to trust in Him to guide you, and not expect all the questions answered up front."

Ethan sighed. He couldn't dispute that theory, but he had to repeat, "We're like fire and ice, Jon. What happens when you put fire and ice together?" He sighed and hung his head.

Jon was silent a long moment before he said, "Water."

Ethan looked up and Jon added, "The fire melts the ice. The water puts out the fire. They work together, they compromise . . . "

Ethan chuckled, amazed that he actually felt better. "Water," he repeated.

"Now," Jon said, "I think we should go inside and have breakfast. I don't know about you, but I'm hungry. Besides, my sister's worried about you."

"She is?" Ethan asked, feeling some hope that she might actually, one day, feel some of what he felt for her.

"Yes, Ethan, I believe she is."

Everyone was nearly finished eating when they came into the kitchen. Ethan's heart quickened when Sara looked his way. He nodded and smiled, but then tried to avoid looking at her, fearing she might somehow sense what he was feeling. He concentrated instead on observing the children with the new baby, and he was glad to see that Maddie was looking well, even vibrant. He thought about Sara having to go through the same thing and prayed she would fare as well.

"I think it's Ethan's turn," Jon said after each of the children and Mona had held the baby.

"Oh, no," he said, "I don't think that—"

"Just take her," Jon said, and Mona put the infant into his arms. "She's two weeks old and you've not held her once."

"She won't break," Mona said.

Ethan chuckled tensely and looked into the chubby little face. It only took a minute to get used to the feel of her in his arms, and then he touched her soft face and hair. "She's mighty pretty," he said, "even though I think she looks a bit like you, Jon."

Jon laughed. "She'll grow out of that."

"What's her name again?" Ethan asked.

"Sylvia Anne," Jon said. "The Sylvia's after Maddie's mother, but I think we'll call her Anne so we don't get the two confused."

"Anne," Ethan said to the baby. "I think it's a fine name."

Ethan managed to avoid Sara outside of mealtimes for the rest of the day, just as he had for days. That evening during scripture time, she asked Jon a question that sent them into a discussion on the plan of salvation. Ethan appreciated that Sara showed a keen interest. He had to believe, with what he knew, that in time she would embrace their beliefs. Watching her discreetly, he realized the seeds of his feelings for her were growing and blossoming; that he was coming to accept them in his heart. Perhaps what frightened him most was the reality that he *wanted* it to work out. He didn't know how it could, but he had to believe the Lord knew what He was doing. And he genuinely *wanted* to be with this woman forever.

Ethan forced himself to focus on what Jon was saying. At a brief lull he ventured to add, "But you know what I think is the most wonderful part of God's plan for us? The Atonement."

He tried not to notice the way Sara focused on him as she said, "I don't understand."

"Well," he said, mostly looking down, "the thing is, I'd heard all about Jesus and that He died for our sins and all that when I was a kid. When I joined the Church there were a lot of things that made more sense to me, but it wasn't until I finally started trying to put my life back together last year that it really made sense. Jesus Christ's death was the final step in what He had to do for us. But the important part came in the Garden of Gethsemane, when he suffered for us. What I didn't get before was that . . . well, I knew that he suffered for our sins and mistakes, and that's why we could go back to live with Him and the Father again, even though we're not perfect, but what I understood after I lost Hannah was that He also suffered for our grief and our sorrow. He would have taken the pain from me years ago if I had just been willing to give it to Him. When I finally turned the pain over to Him, I was able to find peace."

Ethan looked up to see tears shining in Sara's eyes. He forced himself not to stare, and finished by saying, "Anyway, that's my favorite part of the plan. I don't know where I'd be otherwise."

Jon broke an awkward silence by continuing on the same avenue. When they finished with prayer and the children had gone up to bed, Ethan struggled for something to say to Sara. He felt he needed to bridge the silence that had continued between them since the night little Anne had been born. He uttered a silent prayer, and was surprised at how quickly the words formed in his mind. He stopped her in the hall.

"Sara," he said and fought against his temptation to feel nervous, "I would like to accept your offer." She looked confused, and he added quickly, "I would love to have you teach me how to read and write." She smiled, and he felt his hope deepen.

"That would be fine," she said. "When would you like to start?"

"Whenever you have the time."

"How about tomorrow right after lunch? Being Sunday, I don't think you have much work to do."

"Right after lunch would be fine," he said, and watched her walk away. He shook his head in disbelief, wondering how he was ever going to get through this.

* * * * *

Sara awoke Sunday morning feeling a definite desire to go to church. The discussion she'd been a part of the previous evening had touched something in her. She thought of all the little things she had learned from Jon and Maddie about their beliefs since Jon had first joined the Church. She'd respected much of what they'd told her, but she'd always felt it was not for her. Her father's ideas on religion had been very shallow, and she'd passively followed his lead. But she was trying to find herself. She felt as if she'd come far in the time she'd been here, and she was intrigued with the idea that perhaps religion was a part of her search.

Feeling physically better than she had since her arrival, Sara arose and looked at the clothes hanging in her closet. She'd come to feel out of place. Her current wardrobe was suitable for the doctor's daughter/attorney's wife that she'd been. That was behind her now. She had quickly come to see the beauty of this place, its people, and the lifestyle around her. And she wanted to fit in. It wasn't that she wanted to lose herself among the crowd, but rather, she instinctively believed that the real her desired the common and practical ways that her brother had adopted. She thought of the changes in him since he'd settled here. He dressed differently, according to his new lifestyle, but no less dignified or tasteful. Sara had a desire to find the woman she really was, and somehow the clothes she had worn in her past were too reminiscent of the woman she no longer wanted to be.

Wearing a long dressing gown, Sara went down the stairs, made certain no one was in the kitchen beyond Mona, and then slipped up the other stairs to Jon and Maddie's room. She found Maddie sitting up in bed, nursing the baby. Jon had gone down to the clinic.

"Good morning," Maddie said brightly. "What can I do for you?"

"Well," Sara said, "I was wondering if I could ask you something."

"Of course. Anything."

Sara briefly explained her feelings about her wardrobe, and how it represented who she no longer wanted to be. She concluded by asking, "So, until I can get some new clothes . . . do you think I could borrow a few things? We're not built terribly different, and—"

"Oh, you're welcome to anything I've got," Maddie insisted. "In fact, all of those maternity dresses are not going to get used for a long while yet—if ever," she groaned. Sara laughed and Maddie continued, "So go ahead and take them. By the time you have your baby we can get you some new things."

"Oh, thank you," Sara said, glancing through the dresses hanging in Maddie's closet. "They're very nice. You have such good taste."

"You're joking," Maddie said.

"No, really," Sara insisted.

"I've always felt so simple and backward compared to you, Sara."

Sara felt astonished and quickly said, "Oh, Maddie, you've always been such a lady in your own right. You're an example and an inspiration to me."

Maddie actually got tears in her eyes, and Sara sat on the edge of the bed to embrace her. "I'll forever be grateful," Sara said, "for the influence you've had on Jon, and me." She smiled brightly, "In fact, I think I'll be going to church today. You did say you would be going now that you've recovered, and I just . . . would like to see what it's all about."

Maddie laughed between her tears and hugged Sara tightly. Sara basked in her sister-in-law's sweet presence, and felt herself coming a little closer to the woman she needed to be.

* * * * *

Ethan almost choked on his milk when Sara announced at the

breakfast table that she would be going to church with them.

"Phillip's been wanting to go as well," she said, and the child smiled brightly. "I thought we should join you."

"So, how about you, Mona?" Jon asked. "You want to brave it, as well?"

"I certainly don't want to be here all by myself," she stated. "I'd love to go."

As soon as breakfast was over, Ethan took Jon aside and said quietly, "You know those clothes you gave me to wear to church?"

"Yes."

"Well, I really like them, and I like the way it feels to wear them, but I want to know . . . honestly, do I look all right in them? Because I don't want to look like some kind of fool, trying to be something I'm not inside, or—"

"Ethan," Jon said, putting a hand on his arm, "you look great in them. And that's not just my opinion. Maddie has said the same thing. I've told you before that we could go buy you some clothes, if you like. That money you've been earning is adding up."

"No, you just hold onto it. I might need it for something important."

He moved to leave, but Jon stopped him. "Wait a minute. You seem terribly concerned about something. What's on your mind?" When Ethan hesitated, Jon added, "Come on. Talk to me. As I see it, we're practically brothers."

Ethan stared at Jon as the words, and their potential reality, settled into him. Then he laughed. "Well, I'll be," Ethan said, "if only you'd known what you were getting into when your wife invited me to lunch."

Jon grinned and slapped him lightly on the shoulder. "Best thing that's happened to us in years."

"I would think it's the other way around."

"So, tell me what's on your mind, Ethan. You're trying to change the subject."

It didn't take any effort for Ethan to recall his concerns. "It's just that . . . she's so fine and educated. I feel so . . . Oh, I don't know how to say it. But look at me."

"Now, you listen," Jon said. "The thing that both you and my sister need to learn is that background and appearances do not make the person. You are one of the most polite, well-mannered people I have ever known."

Ethan was surprised to see that he really meant it. He felt humble and self-conscious, but somehow grateful as he admitted, "My mama wouldn't put up with bad manners."

"Your mama must have been an angel."

"Yes, sir," he said. "In fact, I'd say she still is."

They both laughed at the implication, then Jon said, "So stop worrying about silly things and just be yourself. Everything will be fine."

Ethan sighed and tried to convince himself that Jon was right. But he couldn't recall ever being so nervous in his entire life.

* * * * *

Sara absorbed her reflection in the long mirror and smiled. She liked the woman looking back at her. In contrast, she realized that there hadn't been a day since she'd married Harrison that she'd been able to like herself. She had been a woman hiding from the truth, and pretending to be something she wasn't. She had indulged in depression, shutting herself away from her problems rather than facing them. But now she'd been given a second chance, and this time she was going to do it right.

She went downstairs with Phillip's hand in hers and found Jon there with Lizzy and Hansen. Mona was smoothing Lizzy's hair into a ribbon. Jon said, "Maddie will be down in a minute, and then we can go."

She was about to ask where Ethan was when he appeared from the hallway. She caught her breath unexpectedly as he met her eyes. She realized now that she'd never seen him coming or going on his way to church. He looked so perfectly natural dressed in the fine black suit, that she could hardly imagine him as he usually dressed—in faded overalls. The contrast was almost breathtaking. She couldn't resist complimenting him. "You clean up well, Mr. Caldwell." She smiled, hoping he wouldn't take offense.

She saw him taking in her simple dark dress and white lace collar, then his eyes met hers again before he smiled. "Thank you," he said. "And I must say that simplicity suits you . . . Mrs. Hartford. I doubt that the two of you have ever looked prettier."

Sara laughed softly when she caught his meaning, and absently rubbed her hand over her well-rounded belly. She didn't know how any man could think she was attractive in this condition, but there was something in Ethan Caldwell's eyes that made her feel more beautiful than she ever had.

Going to church was even more pleasurable than Sara had imagined it could be. She'd met a few people previously on her trips into town. Everyone went out of their way to make her feel welcome, and fussed over her almost as much as the new baby. Throughout the service, Sara's burgeoning interest in Ethan Caldwell—in his Sunday best—almost rivaled her interest in the service. All things considered, she felt more alive and aware than she ever had in her life. Turning to her newly acquired habit of personal prayer, Sara silently uttered words of gratitude, *Thank you for bringing me here. And please, keep us all safe and well.* With any luck, she thought, the past would never catch up with her.

* * * * *

Ethan's hope for the future blossomed as he observed Sara Hartford sitting in church, dressed in a way that made her seem more within his reach. He thought about Jon's point that background and appearance didn't make a person, but he was practical enough to realize that their differences could be a challenge. Still, he was seeing evidence that they were on the right track.

On the way home from church, and through the course of Sunday dinner, Ethan mused on the appointment he had with Sara that afternoon. He almost felt like a kid at Christmas time while he attempted to keep his attention on eating. When the kitchen had been cleaned up, Sara said to him, "I'll meet you in the parlor in a few minutes."

Ethan was sitting on the sofa when Sara entered the room carrying a couple of books and a pencil. He stood, and waited to sit back down until she was seated beside him.

"What's that you've got?" she asked, motioning toward the book in his hands.

"When I was about fifteen or so, a good woman took me in. She not only got me through being sick, she taught me about the gospel. She saved my life. She didn't know it then, but years later, long after she'd died, it was the gospel she'd given to me that got me through.

She gave me this book. She used to read to me out of it, but I always wanted to learn to read so that I could read it myself."

"Well, let's get started then," she said. "You'll be reading before you know it."

She opened one of the books, and he could see now that it was filled with blank paper. She started writing letters and he said, "I know the alphabet and the sounds they make. I just never learned to put them together very well."

She smiled with genuine pleasure and said, "That's a good start then. So, let's just go over them quickly."

They laughed often as they sounded out the letters together, and he decided that being uneducated had never been so enjoyable.

"Very good," she said, concluding that he did indeed know the letters very well. She went over some examples of putting the sounds together, and he felt like he finally had a feel for how reading worked. They took a break so that Sara could spend some time with Phillip, while Ethan went over the things she'd written in the book, practicing what she'd taught him. When they resumed a couple hours later, she was amazed at his progress and commented on how much he already knew and how quickly he was learning.

"Now, let's take a look at that book." He handed it to her and she looked at the cover. "The Book of Mormon," she said. "I've heard Jon and Maddie talk about this, and I assume we've been reading some out of this for scripture study. I must admit to being curious." She smiled. "We can explore the book together."

Ethan smiled in return. He couldn't think of anything better than that.

"Go ahead and try it," she said and pointed to a place on the page where she wanted him to start.

Ethan took a deep breath and began to read, "I . . ." He squinted and looked at the next word carefully. "Well, if that isn't the silliest word I ever saw. Nep-hi. Who in the world is Nep-hi?"

"No," Sara laughed softly, "whenever you put a p with an h, the two letters together sound like an f. So, that word is Nephi."

"Oh, Nephi!" he said and laughed. "I know him." He cleared his throat and began again. "I, Nephi, ha . . ." he struggled to sound it out and she helped him. "Having been born of . . . goodly . . .

parents." He smiled and said, "I like that part. I was born of goodly parents you know. They had their struggles and such; we all do, for sure. But still, they were goodly parents."

Sara looked up at him and found herself staring into his eyes. She had to agree. "Yes, I was born of goodly parents, as well. It would seem we have something in common after all . . . Ethan."

"It would seem that we do," he said, and then forced himself to look back at the book. While he was enjoying their time together, the fact that she was teaching him made him feel like a child. He found it difficult to comprehend being her protector and provider. *Provider?* The very idea was preposterous. She had enough money to buy land and have a house built on it without even blinking. He was working for his room and board and a little cash to set aside.

"Ethan," she said, startling him, "are you all right?"

"Just a little tired, I guess," he said.

"Well, we've come far in one day. You've done well. We'll just keep working on it."

"Thank you," he said and came to his feet, suddenly needing to talk to Jon. "I'll see you at supper."

"Of course," she said, almost sounding disappointed.

Ethan found Jon sitting in his bedroom with a book.

"How you doing?" he asked quietly.

"Good," Jon said. "And you?"

"I'm all right, I guess." He leaned his shoulder against the doorframe.

"What's on your mind, Ethan?" he asked.

"What makes you think something's on my mind?"

Jon raised an eyebrow in suspicion, and Ethan knew there was little good in avoiding the truth.

"All right, fine." He entered the room and sat on the edge of the bed. "I've just been thinking about . . . what we talked about before and . . . I don't know what to think. I've only known her for little more than two weeks. I feel like my whole life has turned upside down. When I fell for Hannah, it was . . . well, we got to know each other. We liked each other. I courted her. We planned the wedding. It was . . . slow. It was kind of, well, our feelings evolved naturally. So . . . why this great manifestation now? Why is it necessary for me to know *now?* It kind of scares me."

"Well," Jon said, "I certainly can't answer those questions, and neither can you. But I would bet that one day you'll understand."

"I hope so, because I sure don't understand right now. I mean . . . she's beautiful, and I'm learning that she truly is a good woman, but . . . I feel like a child when I'm with her. There she is teaching me to read, and I'm trying to imagine myself being her protector and provider. I can't provide for her."

"She doesn't need money to live, that's true. But she needs a man to do all of the things a man does. She'd never survive out here without hired help."

"Well, maybe that's it. I feel like I should be her hired help . . . and I'm actually contemplating being her husband. It's insane."

"Ethan," Jon said, "we're back to the same point we came to earlier."

"Okay," Ethan said, "but . . . how does the saying go? A bird and a fish might fall in love, but where are they going to live?"

Jon shrugged his shoulders and said, "Maybe they'd build a floating nest."

Ethan chuckled and shook his head. "There we are, back to water again."

"Ethan," Jon leaned forward and spoke carefully, "just take it one day at a time, and don't worry so much about what you believe the outcome will be. Get to know her. Let her get to know you. The two of you are very different, yes. But in many ways, Maddie and I have the same differences. Our upbringings were drastically different. But we fell in love quickly. We overcame the obstacles. We're happy together. You have so much to offer her. She has a lot to offer you. When you look at this in the right perspective, it's love and respect and commitment that make a relationship work. So, as you each learn, and compromise, and grow closer together, you'll find the place where your hearts can meet."

Ethan allowed Jon's words to settle as he lay in bed staring into the darkness above him. He prayed that he would be guided in the steps he should take, that he would have courage to take those steps, and that his life might actually turn out the way he was beginning to hope it would. Feeling some measure of peace, he finally slept.

CHAPTER 6

Fools Together

At breakfast Ethan announced, "I'm going into town this morning, Jon, to get the things at the mill you wanted, and some items at the general store. If anybody wants anything, get it on the list."

Half an hour after he'd finished eating, Ethan had a list in his pocket and the horses harnessed to the sleigh. The day was cold, but not miserably so, with bright skies. The scenery made him pause and contemplate how the snow just seemed to make a blue sky bluer. He jumped onto the seat just before he heard a feminine voice ask, "May I come along?"

Ethan turned to see Sara wearing her long wool coat, gloves, and a long scarf wrapped over her head and around her throat. A folded quilt was draped over one arm.

"If you need something in town, I'd be happy to get it for you."

"What I need is to get out of the house. But I don't want to impose on you if—"

"Some company would be nice." He jumped down and offered a hand to help her up. Something warm rushed through him as her gloved hand met his. He helped her onto the seat and sat beside her while she arranged the quilt over her lap.

"It's a big blanket," she said, "if you'd like to share."

"No thank you, ma'am," he said. "I've got my long underwear on." She looked surprised and he chuckled. "Oh, forgive me. It's probably not suitable to say such things in front of a lady such as yourself."

"On the contrary," she said. "I appreciate the way you're so down to earth. It's so . . . refreshing."

He smiled at her as the horses started forward. They rode for several minutes in silence before Ethan said, "So, now that you've been here a while, what do you think? Do you still want to settle here for good?"

"Oh, I do!" she said eagerly. "I love it here."

"It must be so different than what you're used to," Ethan said.

"Yes, but . . . it reached a point where everything in Boston had become so . . . stifling. I felt almost suffocated, somehow. Being here makes me feel like . . . like I can breathe freely. I can be myself."

"I take it then that you've found yourself," he said. She looked confused. "You did say you had come here to find yourself. I just wondered if you'd been able to do that."

"Well," she said, inhaling deeply, "perhaps not completely. But I feel like I'm on the right path, and I've made some glorious first steps."

"That's good then," Ethan said. "But don't find yourself too quickly. Life might get dull if you don't have any discoveries left to make."

Her smile was beautiful and he had to consciously will himself to watch the road ahead. "So," he said, "tell me about Boston. I've never seen a big city before."

"Never? Not even Salt Lake City?"

"Nope. Never been there, but then, I understand it's not much compared to Boston."

"Well, we spent some time in Salt Lake City when we came out last year for vacation. It's nice, but Boston is very different. It's on the waterfront, for one thing. I loved looking out over the Atlantic. If I were going to miss anything, I think it would be that. However, the mountains make up for it, I believe." She looked around and inhaled the fresh air again. "I do love the mountains."

"Yes, ma'am. There's nothing like them. I mean, there's mountains where I come from—sort of, but they weren't like this."

"Where *did* you come from?" she asked.

"Arkansas is where I grew up. I came out west when I was about fifteen."

For the remainder of the trip they shared stories of their growing years. Ethan was surprised at how comfortable he felt with her, in spite of the constant jittery feeling in his stomach. His errands were accomplished quickly, although he received speculative glances from people who saw them together in the store—which didn't surprise him. He was a little astonished himself.

On the return trip they continued sharing past experiences, talking and laughing as if they'd been friends forever. Ethan felt deeply comforted and full of hope. Perhaps this arrangement would be workable after all.

When they were nearly home, Ethan asked, "So, when is that baby of yours due?"

"First of the year," she said. "Of course, you never know. It could come any time between Christmas and the middle of January."

"Of course," he said, hoping deep inside that she would get through the ordeal without any difficulties.

When they arrived home Ethan helped Sara down from the sleigh, expecting her to go in the house, but she hovered close by while he unharnessed the horses, and she then followed him into the barn where he removed their bridles and proceeded to feed them and brush them down. While she chatted about trivial things, he had a feeling there was something she wanted to say. He prayed it would be something that put a positive end to their enjoyable excursion.

Sara watched Ethan urge the horses into their stalls, patting and talking to them in a gentle manner that almost defied his rugged appearance. She continued to be fascinated with the contrasts in his nature—the absolute masculinity of a man so tender and good-hearted almost seemed too good to be true. There were moments when she wondered if he *was* too good to be true, but her instincts told her he was exactly what he appeared to be. Unlike Harrison, who was full of pretense and mockery. Being in Ethan's presence was like standing in a summer rain following endless days of scorching heat. She often felt breathless just being near him, her stomach reacting with a giddy lurch. It made her feel somehow like a child; the child she'd never fully allowed herself to be.

Sara ran out of the small talk that was easing her nerves. Ethan glanced toward her expectantly and she could almost believe he had the ability to read her mind. He seemed to know that there was more behind her chatter than idle conversation or just passing the time. She cleared her throat carefully and forced herself to express the thoughts that had been with her—far more than she cared to admit.

"I really enjoyed our little excursion," she said. "I must say it's eased some of my doubts and . . ."

While she struggled to find the right words, he looked toward her, his brow furrowed. "Doubts?" he echoed.

"Well," she continued while he brushed one of the horses, occasionally glancing toward her, "I have to admit that there have been times since I came here that I've felt comfortable with you, and we've been able to talk, but . . . there are other times when I feel certain that you don't like me at all." He abruptly stopped brushing, his expression betraying alarm. "What I mean is that . . . I realize when I first came here, I wasn't necessarily kind, but . . . we've already talked about that, I know. I guess what I want to know is . . . well . . ." She pulled her shoulders back and lifted her chin. "I just want to know where I stand with you, Ethan. Because . . . if you think I'm not worth your time and attention, I'd just like to know now, instead of continuing to wonder."

He took a step toward her and opened his mouth to speak, but she held up her hands to stop him. "No. Before you say anything, you should know that I want you to be completely honest with me. I mean . . . I wouldn't expect you to ever be anything but honest, and you weren't afraid to tell me what you thought of me before, but . . . I still think you might be kind enough to spare my feelings, and I don't want you to spare my feelings. I want to know exactly where we stand because . . . well, I suppose if I'm asking that of you, then you have the right to know exactly where I stand. And the thing is . . . I think you're a good man, Ethan. I've never known anyone like you. It seems that every man I've known—beyond my brother—has never been quite what he appeared. And I believe that you are exactly what you appear to be. Good, hard-working, sensitive, and . . ." Sara began stammering and embarrassment took over. She felt her cheeks turn warm. She glanced down, not wanting him to see her blush. But she immediately concluded that she had to get it over with, or she might never get up the courage again. A quick glance told her he was now speechless.

"I told you I came here to find myself, and the truth is, you've helped me do that. I want you to know that I respect and admire you, and I want to be the kind of person that you would respect and admire, as well, so . . ."

Sara felt her words run out completely. The silence became thick and she felt embarrassed for rambling on so openly. "Listen to me running on," she said, wringing her gloved hands. "You just have this way—without even trying—of just . . . making words run out of my mouth until I'm gushing all over the place and making a fool of myself and—"

"Is that what you're doing?" he asked, a subtle humor in his eyes, though she couldn't discern if his humor was meant to ease the tension or mock her. "Making a fool of yourself? It sounded more to me like you were pouring your heart out. And being the kind of man you'd pour your heart out to is probably the best thing I've ever been."

He put his hands on his hips, his gaze full of meaning. She had to turn away. She became so focused on her breathing that she didn't hear him moving toward her. She gasped to feel his hands on her shoulders, and to hear his whispered words so close to her ear. "Sara . . . Oh, Sara . . ."

Ethan paused long enough to realize what he was doing. He wondered where this sudden burst of courage had come from, and it only took a moment for him to figure it out. Did the good Lord know him so well? Without the witness from the Spirit that had led him to believe Sara Hartford was right for him, he would never have been able to let go of the mind-set that they were simply too different. He would have assumed her interest in him was a passing fancy. He would have remained certain that the best thing for both of them was distance, and then he would have left, once and for all. As it was, he could only feel grateful that she'd taken the first step in bridging the chasm between their worlds. He closed his eyes and inhaled the sweet fragrance of her hair, thanking God for putting him here at this time, with this opportunity before him. And he prayed with all his heart that their story would have a happy ending.

He briefly thought of Hannah, and wondered if he was a fool to open his heart again. Fear crept in, tempting him to believe that he *was* simply being a fool, that there was no bridge wide enough to close the gap between them. But he felt her shoulders tremble in his hands, and heard her breathing sharpen. His desire to be near her overrode all else and he subtly eased closer.

Sara held her breath as Ethan slid his hands slowly down her arms and back up again. She closed her eyes and exhaled as he meekly pressed his lips into her hair. The moment became so dreamlike that she had to turn and face him, if only to verify that the experience was real. His eyes delved into hers as if he could see right through to her soul. The intensity of his gaze was almost too much, and she nearly looked away, but her desire to see into *his* soul kept her focus equally intent. He lifted a hand to touch her face, pausing only long enough to remove his glove. His fingers smelled of warm leather.

"Tell me I'm a fool," he murmured, while she concentrated on the rough, calloused feel of his fingers. "Tell me I'm crazy to be thinking what I'm thinking. Tell me, Sara, and I'll believe you. Tell me I'm a fool and I'll leave here and never come back."

"Oh, you mustn't do that," she said, impulsively removing her own glove to touch his stubbled face.

"Why not?" he asked, his voice deepening.

Inspired by the honesty of the moment, Sara felt compelled to say, "Because it would be more foolish for us to be apart and alone, when we could be fools together."

His face broke into a wide grin, deepening the lines at the corners of his eyes.

"Is something funny, Mr. Caldwell?" she asked.

"No, ma'am," he said with a little chuckle. "It's just that I've spent a lot of years just being a lonely old fool. Being fools together sounds awfully appealing."

Sara watched his smile soften with his eyes. Her heart quickened further as she sensed his desire to kiss her. She was wondering what she'd ever done to deserve such a man coming into her life when she heard a noise at the door. Ethan stepped back only a second before the door flew open. The children came running in, full of laughter.

"We made a snowman," Lizzy announced. "And he has a real hat and a carrot nose and raisin buttons. Come see. Come see."

Ethan shot Sara an amused glance before they trudged through the snow and around the house to see the snowman. Afterward he went back to unload the sleigh while she went in the house with the children. Over lunch nothing appeared any different. But Sara glanced often at Ethan's eyes, reminding her that something warm and wonderful had awakened between them. She was almost afraid to admit to all of her thoughts—the idea that he could solve her every problem made her feel ashamed and guilt ridden. She knew what she felt for him was real and deep, and that it was independent of the fact that he had what she needed. But if he knew the truth about her past, she felt certain he would misinterpret her apparent motives, and that would drive him away forever. She could only pray that the truth would remain concealed long enough for him to know that her heart was in the right place. Or perhaps the truth could remain concealed forever.

The children ate quickly, then went to see if their mittens and stockings, hung by the stove, had dried. They were soon outside again while the adults hovered about the table, visiting casually. A knock at the door sent Maddie to answer it. She returned with an envelope in her hand. "A telegram," she announced.

"I hate telegrams," Jon said. "I've only gotten two before now, and I bet you can guess what they were because you sent both of them." He pointed at Sara with a mocking scowl that made her laugh.

"This one isn't for you," Maddie said, and handed the envelope to Sara. Even before she opened it, she knew that her prayer had come too late. The truth was about to unfold, and there was nothing she could do about it.

Ethan watched Sara's hands tremble as she opened the envelope and read the telegram. He saw the horror in her eyes just before she lifted them to meet Jon's. Jon looked back, his expression full of concern.

"What is it?" he demanded. "What's happened?"

Sara held the telegram out toward Jon, who took it hesitantly, then read. Sara's eyes turned toward Ethan, and he saw a regret there that burned right through him. Then she turned away, her expression stricken with shame.

"What does it say?" Maddie asked quietly.

Jon didn't even hear, but said, "What does this mean?"

Ethan felt his chest tighten, and his palms began sweating as he watched Sara's trembling. He wanted to hold her in his arms and soothe away whatever had upset her. Then he realized that their friendly little exchange in the barn did not automatically make him privy to a family crisis.

"Excuse me," he said, coming to his feet. "Perhaps it would be more appropriate if I left you to—"

"No," Sara said abruptly and took hold of his arm. Her voice softened as she added, "You need to hear this, too." Ethan sat back down. Sara closed her eyes and took a deep breath. She opened them and spoke in a voice that was barely steady. "I . . . have reason to believe that my husband's business dealings were not . . . entirely legal."

Jon's eyes widened as Maddie gasped. Mona was the only one who didn't look surprised. Ethan did his best to keep a neutral expression on his face as she went on. "I don't believe that . . . his death was an accident."

Maddie gasped again and clapped a hand over her mouth. Jon's face reddened in anger, but Mona stared at Sara with deep compassion in her eyes. Sara glanced briefly at Ethan before she looked down and finished firmly, "I believe that whoever is responsible will . . . come after my money."

Jon asked tersely, "You believe it *now?* Or you believed it before you came here?"

Sara's trembling increased as she said, "I knew . . . before he was killed that . . . that something was terribly wrong. After his death I put the pieces together and . . ." She became too emotional to speak and pressed a hand over her mouth, but it didn't begin to muffle the cries she could no longer suppress. Ethan watched her helplessly, hating the distance between them when he could almost feel her pain.

"What does it say?" Maddie repeated, motioning toward the telegram. Jon passed it to Maddie, whose eyes widened as she read. Ethan wanted desperately to know what it said, but he knew he wouldn't be able to read it without great effort, even if he could see it. He was relieved beyond expression when Maddie read it aloud. *"I know where you are. I'm coming for what's rightfully mine."* She stared at it as if she couldn't believe her eyes, and then said gently to Sara, "Tell us what you know. Who is this?"

Sara sniffed and wiped her face with a lacy white handkerchief. "I don't know anything that could incriminate me, or even make my knowledge a threat to anyone else. And what I do know is little beyond suspicion, but . . . I believe that Harrison was involved in some kind of illegal investment, something went wrong, and some people out there think he owes them a great deal of money. When he didn't pay it, they killed him. His death was declared an accident, but the evidence implies otherwise."

"Did you tell the police all of this?" Jon asked tersely.

"Yes, I told them everything I knew. And they suggested that I go ahead and do what I'd been wanting to do for months."

"What's that?" Jon asked.

"Leave," Sara stated, and Jon's eyes widened. "That's right, Jon, I was ready to leave him. He treated me worse than he treated his dog. I'd had enough. I was ready to come out here and beg you to let me stay with you. I knew if I did I would lose practically everything. Legally, everything I had became his when we married. But I was willing to work hard, to do whatever I had to to take care of myself and Phillip. And then I found out I was pregnant. The uncertainty was too risky with a baby coming. I couldn't bring myself to come out here and become a burden on you and your family. When he was killed I sold everything as quickly as I could and made my escape. Knowing they might come after me for the money only made me determined to come more quickly. So there, that's it. Now you know the truth."

"I can't believe it," Jon said angrily.

Sara retorted firmly, "What can't you believe, Jon? That my husband was a despicable wretch? That I would be so despicable myself as to be absolutely relieved at my husband's death? Or that I came here and put your home and family in danger? What is it that you can't believe?"

Jon put his hand over hers and softened his voice. "I can't believe you didn't tell me the truth . . . right from the start. How long you were living in absolute misery without letting us know. I don't care how destitute you might have been, we would have taken care of you. And why didn't you tell us what was going on when you came? Did you think the problem would just go away?"

"Maybe I did," she said, her emotion rising again. "But whoever's behind this is not going to make me pay any more for Harrison's mistakes. I've already paid a price higher than you could possibly imagine. I sacrificed my dignity, my self-respect, and my happiness for that man. And I'm not paying *anybody* a single penny. That money is my security for my children's future, and I *won't* give it up!" She rose abruptly and moved to leave, but she'd only taken a few steps when she hesitated and teetered. Ethan shot to his feet just as she collapsed, barely managing to catch her.

"Good heavens," Maddie cried, realizing Sara had passed out.

Jon quickly checked her vitals, then reported, "She's fine. I think she just stood up too fast. Being as pregnant as she is didn't help."

"I'll take her upstairs and sit with her," Ethan said.

"Thank you," Jon said, "I'll be up in a few minutes."

Ethan nodded and headed up the stairs, certain that Jon wanted an opportunity to speak candidly with Mona about the situation. He laid Sara on her bed. She stirred slightly and opened her eyes, looking disoriented.

"It's all right," he said. "I think you need to rest."

She nodded, and he covered her with a crocheted blanket that was folded at the foot of the bed. With her eyes closed she reached a hand toward him and said, "Please stay with me, Ethan."

He took hold of her hand and squeezed it tightly. "I promise," he said and she quickly drifted to sleep.

Ethan let go of her hand only long enough to move a chair close to the edge of the bed. He sat down and gently held her long fingers between his. He wondered at their softness, impulsively pressing the back of her hand to his lips. While she slept he silently prayed. His mind played through everything he'd just learned, and he felt surprisingly calm. Somehow he knew that everything would be all right. And he knew because he'd been told in no uncertain terms, straight from the top, that he was here to be her protector. And he would be! He would lay down his own life before he would allow anything to happen to her or her son. And he knew that the Spirit would guide him in seeing to her safety, just as it had guided him to this point. He marveled at how his faith had been strengthened through the experience. And now, as he absorbed the entire picture, he knew what he needed to do. He didn't even have to wonder. Of course, Sara would have to decide what *she* wanted. All he could do was offer, and pray that all would be well in the end.

Ethan became distracted from his thoughts when Jon entered the room and sat on the edge of the bed, setting his crutches beside him. He pressed his fingers to Sara's throat for a few seconds, then briefly touched her brow. He turned to look at Ethan, and Ethan felt some questions coming, but Sara stirred awake and they both focused their attention on her.

"How are you?" Jon asked.

"I'm all right . . . relatively speaking," she said, and then her eyes turned to Ethan. The hope he saw there barely glimmered through her obvious regret and shame. She glanced briefly toward Jon while she squeezed Ethan's hand. He suspected there was something she wanted to tell him, but not while her brother was there.

"Sara," Jon said, "I don't want you to get upset again, but . . . there's something I have to say."

"I'm fine," she insisted and sat up, leaning against the headboard. Ethan loved the way she kept her hand in his.

"First of all," Jon continued, "we're going to take every precaution to keep you and Phillip safe. Maddie's already gone with her father to talk to the local authorities. We'll keep the children with us every minute. We'll keep the doors locked, even during the days. We won't take any chances. I want Ethan to stay in the empty room up here, so he can be close by." He looked at Ethan as if for approval, and Ethan nodded firmly. "And I think it's good that Phillip has been sleeping in Hansen's room, under the circumstances."

"Of course," Sara said.

"Now," Jon said, "with that made clear, I want you to know that I'm not angry with you. I'm angry at the circumstances you're in, Sara. I would do anything for you—anything. I want you to be happy and safe and well. And I'll do whatever it takes to see that you are. With that in mind, I just have to say that . . . I understand your feelings about the money, Sara, but . . ." Sara visibly tensed, but Ethan didn't feel concerned. He already knew what the answers were, and he knew that everything would be all right.

"But?" Sara pressed.

"We can find a way to provide for your needs, Sara. There are other options. Don't let pride and fear make you hold onto something that could put you in danger. If Harrison is dead over this money, then you have to know that this is serious. Please, carefully consider what's best."

"I appreciate your concern, Jon, but do you really think that wouldn't have occurred to me before now? I've thought it through a thousand times. And if you must know, I've prayed about it." His eyes widened. "That's right, your sister has been praying—a great deal, in fact. I can't explain how I know, Jon, but I *know* that I need to keep that money. I firmly believe that with it I can make a difference in this community. I don't know exactly how yet, but I'm going to find out. And I'm not giving my money to some criminal lowlife."

Jon sighed. "I hear what you're saying, Sara, but you said you know very little of the situation. What if this someone who's after you is *legally* entitled to the money, because it's technically Harrison's money? What then?"

Sara looked down abruptly. "I don't know, Jon. I don't have all the answers. I just know that I have to hold my ground."

Jon sighed again, more deeply. "Okay. Well, that's all I have to say." He took up his crutches and stood with their help. "Ethan, when you get a minute, I've got some firearms that might give us some leverage. You can take your pick of whatever suits you best."

Ethan nodded. "Thank you. That would be good, I think, as long as you talk to the kids about what's going on and that they need to keep away from the guns."

"I'll do that right now," Jon said and left the room.

Ethan turned to find Sara looking directly at him. While he was wondering what to say, she spoke firmly. "You must be so disappointed in me . . . so disgusted by the—"

"Don't go telling me how I feel," he retorted gently. "Why would you think I'd be either?"

"I don't know how to explain it. I just feel so . . ." Tears brimmed in her eyes and she looked away apologetically. "I'm so sorry, Ethan."

Ethan touched her chin and turned her face back to his view. He wiped at her tears as he said, "Now, what have you got to be apologizing for? This wasn't your doing, Sara."

"Then why do I feel so guilty? Why do I feel like I must have done something wrong somewhere along the way?"

Ethan sighed and took both her hands into his. "You know, I think that's the question that made it most difficult for me in getting over Hannah's death. I felt sure that she had died as some kind of . . . punishment for me. I felt certain if I'd just had more faith, or been a better person, or *something,* that it wouldn't have happened that way. Eventually I learned that sometimes bad things just happen, and we have to make the most of them. I don't see that you have anything to be ashamed of, and certainly nothing to be sorry for."

She pressed a hand to the side of his face. "You're so sweet, Ethan, but . . . at the very least, I should have been more honest with you. I should have told you the truth."

"You had no reason to," he said. "Until a few hours ago, I don't think either of us had any logical reason to think that we were anything more than casual acquaintances."

Sara looked into his eyes with hope so tangible he could almost touch it. "And what are we now, Ethan, if we're not casual acquaintances?"

Ethan blew out a long, slow breath. "Well, that's something I wanted to talk to you about."

Sara hardly dared breathe. She felt certain that he would tell her, in spite of his compassion and understanding, that he simply didn't want to have any personal involvement with her now. She was amazed at how much the very idea hurt her. How had she come to care for and trust him so completely in such a short time?

"I have a lot of thoughts going around in my mind," he said, "and a lot of feelings tied into them, so I hope I can make sense of all that and say what I need to say. And I hope you'll be patient with me while I get it all sorted out."

"Of course," she said.

Ethan hesitated when they heard a child's footsteps coming up the stairs. Lizzy bounded into the room announcing, "Mama says that supper's ready and to come right away."

"Thank you, Lizzy," Ethan said, and she left just as quickly. "It can wait a while," he added to Sara, but she wanted to protest. As hungry as she felt, her anxiety over what he had to say was far worse. He came to his feet and said, "Would you rather I brought something up for you?"

"No, thank you," she said. "I'm fine." He held her hand while she came to her feet, and he kept her elbow in his hand as they walked down the stairs, as if he wanted to be certain she wouldn't lose her balance. But he let go once they entered the kitchen, and she wondered if he had a problem showing his affection for her in front of the family.

The meal passed with minimal conversation and a tension in the air, but it seemed lost on the children as they chattered among themselves. Sara felt grateful, as always, for how well Phillip got along with Lizzy and Hansen. There was rarely any contention among them, and she found it one more blessing of being there.

Sara was the first to rise from the table. "I think I'll go lie down again," she said, feeling drained.

"Of course," Maddie said. "Do you want me to get you for scripture study?"

"Uh . . ." She met Ethan's eyes. "Not tonight, thank you. I think I need some time."

She felt hopeful that he'd gotten the point when he stood as well and said, "I'm going to hurry and see to the evening chores. Thank you for supper. It was delicious, as always."

Ethan hurried out the door before Sara even got to the stairs. A quick glance in her direction was the only indication she had that he might know how anxious she felt to resume their conversation.

Sara sat in the chair by the bed and removed her shoes. She rubbed her swelling feet and lifted them onto the edge of the bed. The events of the day tumbled through her mind, making her wonder how something could feel so right and go so wrong in such a short time. She prayed that Ethan would hurry, and that what he wanted to tell her would not be devastating. And she prayed with all her heart that this mess could be undone without bringing any harm to herself or those she loved.

CHAPTER 7

Water

Sara became lost in thought and was actually surprised at the sound of footsteps on the stairs. They could only belong to Ethan; they were too heavy to belong to a woman or child, and Jon was on crutches. Her heart quickened even before he appeared in the doorway. She was in awe of the way his presence could light up a room, even with the severe countenance he bore.

"They're all gathering for scripture study. I told them there was something I needed to do, unless this isn't a good time."

"I've been hoping you'd hurry back," she admitted, and he smiled faintly. She watched him move the other chair in the room closer, and he sat to face her, remaining on the edge of his seat.

He cleared his throat and said in a careful voice, "As I was saying, I have so much on my mind that I hope I can put it together to make sense." He chuckled tensely. "I don't even know where to begin."

"Just say what you have to say," she said. "If it doesn't make sense, I'll let you know."

He nodded, seeming relieved by the idea. "Well, the thing is," he began, "it doesn't take much to see that you and me are from different molds. I've never even been around such a fine lady, and I wouldn't have expected one to actually want to be around *me*. But you asked me earlier to let you know where we stand—from my perspective—and I guess that's what I need to tell you. I suppose what's happened in the meantime just makes me understand more why I feel the way I do, and that I need to quit holding back and just let you know what's going on in my heart."

Sara had to tell herself to keep breathing. However, her fears that this would not be what she wanted to hear lessened as he went on.

Looking directly into her eyes, he said, "The truth is, Sara, I felt something powerful for you the moment you stepped off that train. I kept trying to tell myself that I was a fool, and I felt certain that you'd want nothing to do with me. But you've been so kind, and it's become more and more evident to me that you're a good woman."

Sara couldn't hold back her tears. His words touched something in her, a desperate need for validation from a good man—something she hadn't had for as long as she could remember. Ethan smiled compassionately and reached out to wipe her tears before he continued. "Still, I must admit, I thought that setting my sights on a woman like you was ridiculous. I prayed and prayed to just get you out of my head and . . ." She heard his voice crack, and her own emotion tightened in her chest. "The thing is . . . I don't know if you understand how the Lord can speak to us through our minds . . . and our feelings . . . but I just had to change the way I looked at all of this when . . ." His voice betrayed his emotions. "When it became clear to me that what I felt was right. I wondered why my feelings would be so strong. I even talked to Jon about it."

Sara felt her eyes widen, wondering what Jon might know that she didn't. But she said nothing, not wanting to interrupt his momentum.

Ethan reached out and took both her hands into his. He rubbed his thumbs over the back of her hands, and she found that she was growing accustomed to the calloused feel of his fingers. "The thing is," he said, "if the Lord hadn't let me know that I could be the right man for you, I think I would have been just too plain scared to say what I want to say. But before I say it, I think it's important for you to understand that money has nothing to do with it. I think that's one thing that's hung me up on the idea. The truth is, I have nothing to my name beyond my clothes, a tolerable horse, and a little cash that I've earned from your brother on top of my room and board. It would be easy for you to think that I'm here talking to you like this because you've got money and I don't, and I can only hope that you'll believe I'm telling the truth when I say that it means nothing to me. I've never had money, Sara. I know how to work hard to keep food on the table and a roof over my head, but I've had times of great happiness and great sorrow in my life, and money never had anything to do with it. Am I making any sense so far?"

Sara nodded, unable to speak. She had a good idea where this was headed, and the very idea filled her with hope and joy beyond description. He was the answer to her every prayer, and the very fact that he was so thoroughly humble and innocent about it only made her love him more. And yes, she did love him. Her feelings for him had quickly surpassed anything she'd ever felt for Harrison, and she could no longer deny it.

"Okay," he drawled and she could see that he was nervous. She squeezed his hand in an attempt to offer reassurance. His smile verified that it had helped. "The thing is that . . . well, I've realized just in the last few hours that this money thing really doesn't make much difference, because it's evident that what you *do* have could be gone if we're not careful. I've also realized that . . ." He hesitated as if he were having trouble finding the right words.

He leaned forward and his voice softened in contrast to the way his eyes intensified. "Correct me if I'm wrong, Sara, but I have come to realize that eventually you and I will probably end up together. But under the circumstances, sooner would be better. You see, it all became very clear to me when you said earlier that everything you'd had before you married Mr. Hartford became his when you were married. I never knew that such a thing was true. In my experience it's never mattered." He chuckled softly. "Nobody ever had anything to begin with."

He became serious again and continued. "Now, I know that us being together is not necessarily going to guarantee that whoever is after you're money won't get it. But I think it could help protect what rightfully belongs to you, and even if legally it became mine, just between you and me, it would always be yours. And the fact is, I would be in a better position to see that you're protected and cared for. But I wouldn't want you to make such a decision out of fear or need. I'll do everything in my power to protect you whether you accept my offer or not."

Ethan glanced down briefly and she could see that he was reflecting on what he'd said. "So," he added, looking up again, "it's pretty obvious where I'm headed with this. I'm letting you know where I stand, how I feel, and what I'm willing to do. Now, it's up to you to decide how you feel and what *you're* willing to do. You have a good head on your shoulders and a good heart. And I would never venture to make your decisions for you. All I can do is offer what I have. So, that's what I'm doing. As far as things of the world go, I have nothing to give you. But I can give you my protection, my name, and my heart and soul—except for the part that belongs to God. So," he sighed, "I think that about covers what I have to say. As long as all of that makes sense . . ."

She nodded, fearing that the overpowering emotion building inside of her would burst if she attempted even a sound. She watched him take a deep breath and draw back his shoulders, then in one agile movement he pushed his chair back, went down on one knee, and took her hand into his. "Sara," he began in a shaky voice, "will you marry me?"

Sara's emotion erupted with a sharp whimper. She pressed her free hand over her mouth as if she could hold it back. He seemed concerned but went on, "Let me be a father to your children, Sara. And I'll be a good father to them, I swear it. I will do everything in my power to make you happy and see that you're cared for. I promise to accept you as you are, and all I ask is that you do the same for me." He took another deep breath and repeated, "Will you marry me?"

Her emotions refused to be held back any longer as Sara comprehended how he perfectly answered her every concern. Another sharp whimper slipped through the fingers over her mouth. Then another. And another. Ethan's brow creased with concern and she knew she had to let him know the cause. She tried to force the words to her lips, but the full torrent escaped and she could only sob helplessly. She nodded in an attempt to tell him her answer, then she slid to her knees and wrapped her arms around him, pressing her face to his shoulder, crying without restraint. She cried out all of her fears and inner turmoil regarding her circumstances. She'd kept her emotions pent up inside her since Harrison's death—perhaps even before that. And she cried for the contrasting joy and hope she felt now in knowing that everything would be all right. Feeling Ethan's arms come around her, holding her close, she knew that as long as she had him by her side everything would be fine.

Sara cried so long and hard that they ended up sitting on the floor. Ethan leaned back against the bed, while she leaned against his chest until her crying quieted to an occasional sniffle. Neither of them said anything for several minutes after she'd calmed down. The silence seemed to allow them to catch up with all that had been said, and all that they were feeling. She needed no words to tell her how he felt when he tightened his embrace and pressed his lips to her brow. But she still wanted to ask. "I have one question."

"Anything," he murmured as if he would bring her the stars.

"I just want to know the biggest reason you're willing to do this."

"Oh, that's easy," he said in a light tone that eased the tension immensely. "I thought you were going to ask me something hard."

She sat up enough to look into his eyes. "So, answer it."

Ethan's eyes tightened on her and his hand cupped the side of her face. "I love you, Sara Hartford. It makes no sense at all, but that's just the way it is. I love you. I do."

Sara laughed and new tears sprang forth. "Oh, you're not going to cry again," he said with a little chuckle, wiping her cheeks with his fingers.

"I didn't think I'd have any more tears in me," she said.

"Well, you just go ahead and cry all you want," he murmured, and eased her back into his arms, pressing his lips into her hair. "But I would appreciate an answer to *my* question, just so I don't have to wonder if I've made a fool of myself for nothing."

"What question would that be, exactly?" she asked, hoping he would catch the light tone in her voice.

He chuckled and said, "You just want to hear me say it again."

"Yes, I do," she said and looked up at him without moving her head from his shoulder.

He looked into her eyes and tightened his hold on her. "Will you marry me?"

Sara inhaled deeply, as if she could soak in the perfect humility and adoration that radiated from him. She exhaled slowly and reached up to touch his face, "Yes, Ethan. I would be honored to be your wife." He smiled, and she hurried to add, "I'm humbled and awed by all you're offering me, and I promise you that I will do everything in my power to be a good wife to you, and a good mother to *your* children."

His smiled deepened. "No matter how many we have, they'll all be *our* children. I want to be a father to Phillip, and to this one." He tentatively touched a hand to her rounded belly. "The same as if they were my own."

Sara's vision of him blurred once again with the fresh mist that rose in her eyes. She blinked the tears away and said, "Just remember that the same applies to money, Ethan. Once we're married, it's not mine or yours, it's ours—every last penny of it. And if I end up losing everything, after all that we can do to save it, I know we'll still be all right, because I know that you meant it when you said you would see that we're cared for."

"Yes, ma'am," he said, and she laughed.

"There's just one more thing I need to say," she said firmly.

"What's that?"

"I love you too, Ethan Caldwell. You're the best thing that's ever happened to me."

"Amen," he said just before he kissed her. And with his kiss, it seemed that every unanswered question of her life fell neatly into place. Whatever life brought her from that moment forward, she could never forget how perfectly blessed she was to be loved by such an incredible man.

* * * * *

Ethan helped Sara to her feet and waited a minute while she washed her face and blotted it dry. She smoothed her hair and her dress, then they went together to the parlor where the family was still seated. All eyes turned toward them, but only the adults seemed to notice that they were holding hands. Sara figured now that their feelings had been voiced, it was all right for others to see the evidence of their affection.

"Sorry we're late," Ethan said, sitting in his usual spot. Sara sat beside him, keeping her hand in his.

"You're just in time for prayer," Jon said, looking concerned.

After the prayer was spoken the children hugged everyone and said good night. Jon said to them, "You run along and get all ready for bed. I'll come up to tuck you in in just a few minutes."

Once the children had left the room, all eyes turned expectantly toward Sara and Ethan. Sara was just wondering if she should say something when Ethan spoke up. "Yes," he said, "there's something we need to tell you. I'm sure that's evident. So, I'll just get to the point. Sara and I will be getting married, as soon as we possibly can."

Maddie and Mona looked equally stunned. Jon smiled. Sara recalled Ethan saying that he'd talked to Jon about his feelings, and she wondered what exactly he knew. Sara was relieved when Ethan went on to explain the situation and their feelings on the matter.

"That's incredible," Maddie said when Ethan had finished.

"I can't believe it," Mona added. "I mean it's wonderful, but I just can't believe it."

"It *is* wonderful," Jon said. "In fact, I can't think of anything better than seeing my two favorite people coming together—favorite beyond Maddie and the children, of course." He winked at Maddie.

"Of course," Sara laughed, and she hugged both of them goodnight.

Ethan walked with Sara to kiss Phillip good night, and then walked her to her own room where they sat together for another hour discussing their plans more thoroughly. He left her at the door, saying, "I'm going out to get some of my things, but it will only take a few minutes. I'll be in the next room, and I'm a light sleeper. If I hear anything strange I'll be at your side within seconds, understand?"

She nodded firmly, knowing that such precautions probably weren't necessary. But she felt better, nevertheless, knowing he was there. He touched her face and kissed her in a way that spoke of the hope they shared for a bright future. Sara was asleep before he returned, and she slept soundly with the promise of his love and protection. Her next awareness was the barest hint of daylight in the room, and Ethan's salutations, "Good morning, my love."

She managed to focus on his face and smiled. "Good morning," she said.

"I'm going out to see to the chores in the barn." He wrapped her hand around the cold steel of a pistol. She was suddenly very alert. "Jon told me you know how to use it. I'm locking the door behind me. It's just a precaution, but I don't want to take any chances."

"Thank you," she said. He kissed her brow and slipped out of the room.

* * * * *

Ethan entered the barn and set to work. His light step matched the pleasure and anticipation he felt in his heart. In spite of his lingering concern for Sara's safety, he'd never dreamed that he could be so happy. He'd gotten past trying to logically add up the impossible. His feelings far outweighed any logic. He knew in his heart that he was doing the right thing, and nothing could deter him now. The fact that Sara had reciprocated his feelings seemed to be more than he could ever ask for. Keeping a prayer of gratitude close to his heart, he fed the animals then picked up the milk buckets in order to fill them. As he did so the barn door came open. For a moment he felt nervous, wondering if whoever was looking for Sara had come snooping around. But the quickening of his nerves melted into eager expectation as Sara walked in and closed the door behind her. She glanced at him and smiled before she set aside the pistol he'd given her. Their eyes met for a long moment while he just absorbed her presence, attempting to digest the reality that she would soon be his wife. Her dark hair hung in waves about her shoulders. Beyond the few pre-dawn moments he'd seen her in bed this morning, this was the first time he'd seen her hair when it wasn't coiled and pinned to the back of her head. *She was so beautiful!*

"Forgive me for interrupting your work," she said.

"Don't ever apologize for such a pleasant distraction," he said, and she smiled almost shyly.

"I just . . . had to see you. Lying in bed, thinking about everything that happened yesterday, it began to feel like a dream, and . . . I just had to be certain that it wasn't."

Ethan dropped the empty buckets and moved toward her, compelled by the power of everything he felt for her. "Ethan," she murmured as he drew her fully into his arms. He chuckled and glanced down. The baby she carried prevented him from holding her as close as he'd like to. She smiled as if she understood, and he bent to kiss her. He kissed her as if his life had just begun in this moment, and nothing mattered beyond the need he had to share his future with her. Her response deepened, and he felt her hand press into his hair, holding to him as if he could keep her from falling. When Ethan began to fear that his knees would buckle and they'd both end up losing their balance, he eased back and looked into her eyes.

"I never dreamed . . ." she said in a bare whisper.

"What?" he asked in the same tone.

"That I could feel so . . . loved, so . . . *safe*. And I don't mean your ability to protect me."

"I *know* what you mean," he whispered, and kissed her again. When he began to enjoy it a little too much, he drew away, chuckling as he said, "Careful there, Mrs. Hartford. When I can call you Mrs. Caldwell, you can kiss me like that any time you want."

"I look forward to it," she said and took a step back. "In the meantime, you'd better get your work done. We've got a wedding to plan."

Ethan grinned. "So we do," he said, picking up the milk buckets.

"Can I help?" she asked. At his laugh she said, "What's so funny?"

"I was going to milk the cows and gather the eggs. And I'd bet every dime of that money I'm marrying that you've never been within an arm's length of a cow."

Sara laughed. How he loved to hear her laugh! "You're right about that, but . . . if I can teach you to read and write, surely you can teach me to milk a cow and gather eggs. I mean . . . what will we do one day if you get laid up like Jon is now, and I have to do the chores?"

Ethan laughed. "We'll have Jon come over and do it."

"And what if he can't?" she asked, then added more seriously, "Teach me, Ethan. I want to learn. I want to be capable and strong."

"Oh, I'm not worried about that," he said, "but if you want to learn to milk a cow, I'd be glad to teach you."

Sara kept laughing for no apparent reason as Ethan sat behind her with his arms around her. He was showing her how to squeeze the udder just right to get the milk into the bucket. When she was able to do it alone, she was every bit as pleased with herself as he'd been when he'd read more than two consecutive words. When the milk buckets were full, he showed her how to reach into the chickens' nests to get the eggs. She squealed and pulled her hand back the first time, as if something had bitten her. Then she laughed as she managed to get the eggs with ease.

"Very good," Ethan drawled. "Now if only I could learn to read so quickly."

"Oh, there's no hurry," she said, looking at him directly. "I think I would very much enjoy it if we dragged the lessons out over a long period of time."

"What an excellent idea," Ethan said. She smiled and touched his face.

They went into the kitchen together and washed up while Maddie and Mona were putting breakfast on the table. In the midst of their laughter, Maddie said, "The two of you seem awfully happy."

"Imagine that," Ethan said, and Sara laughed again.

Over breakfast Sara told the children that she would be marrying Ethan, and he would be Phillip's new father. They were all thrilled with the idea—especially Phillip. Sara thought how sad it was that getting over his father's death had taken such little effort. It was a tragedy his father had played such a minimal role in the child's life. The children obviously had no comprehension of how enormously these decisions would affect their lives. They were simply pleased to know that Ethan would be a part of the family forever. Sara wholly agreed.

Right after breakfast Jon and Ethan rode into town to make arrangements for the wedding, while the women talked about the wedding plans and all Sara was feeling. Sara couldn't help being pleased with the absolute support and acceptance she received from the two women. They both meant so much to her.

Ethan returned to announce that all the arrangements had been made, and that they would be getting married the following morning, just as planned.

"Oh my," Sara said and pressed a hand over her quickening heart.

"Any time between now and then you can still change your mind," Ethan said. "After that, you're stuck with me."

She smiled and assured him, "Oh, I won't change my mind. I have too much to gain."

"No, my love," he said, putting his arms around her, "you're the one who's losing all the money. I'm the one who has too much to gain."

"Who said anything about money?" she asked.

He laughed and kissed her; a kiss that made her anticipate being Ethan Caldwell's wife.

The day was busy, full of hasty plans on what Sara would wear, and the meal Mona and Maddie would prepare to celebrate. No one else was invited beyond Maddie's parents and Sara and Jon's aunt and uncle. Ethan took care of notifying them of the event, and they all eagerly agreed to be there.

While Ethan was away from the house on his visits, Sara found a few minutes alone with her brother. They sat together on the sofa and he put his arm around her shoulders.

"So, how are you doing, sweet sister?" he asked.

"I'm doing quite well. How are you?"

"I'm great," he said. "If I could just get rid of this blasted splint."

"All in good time," she said.

"Yes, and I thought that when my foot healed I'd have to let Ethan go. Now we never have to let him go."

"You like that idea?"

"I like it very much. But I have to ask . . . Are you sure this is what you want? Don't think I'm questioning your judgment," Jon said. "I'm not. Ethan's one of the best men I've ever known. I just have to know what you're feeling. This is a big step . . . things are happening very quickly."

"Yes, that's true," Sara said, "and I can't explain how I know that it's right, I just do."

"You don't have to explain. I know what you mean."

"Yes," she smiled, "I'm sure you do. The thing is . . . Ethan makes me feel more alive than I ever have in my life. The very idea actually deepens the sorrow I feel for my past. I didn't know what I was missing. I always assumed that what I felt for Harrison was equivalent to what you felt for Maddie. Now I know I was wrong. When I got here I was envious of your relationship with Maddie, although I still didn't really know what I was missing.

"You know more than anyone how much I loved Father, and I never resented the time I spent working with him, and caring for him. But we both know he had a difficult personality; he was controlling and overprotective. I think I was drawn to Harrison because he was the same way. I was used to being controlled. But it took so little time to see that Harrison did not have the good, caring heart that was beneath Father's crusty exterior. Little by little I felt myself just shriveling up and dying. Well, now I feel alive again. Except I feel that I've never really been alive at all before now. Now I'm doing what I want because I really *want* it. I know I'll be happy because my efforts at keeping my home and being a good wife and mother will be revered and appreciated, instead of being treated as trivial and meaningless. In my opinion, Ethan Caldwell is more of a man than any man I've ever known. Just being with him makes me feel a passion for life and living—and for him—that I never imagined possible." She sighed and realized she was gushing. She finished by saying, "I love him, Jon." Emotion broke her voice. "I realize that I never knew what love really was, and I will forever be grateful to have discovered such feelings now."

Jon smiled widely, and she demanded, "What's funny?"

"Nothing's funny," Jon said. "It's just that . . . you didn't say a single word about the money. Let's just say I'm glad to know your heart's in the right place."

Sara smiled and had to agree, "Yes, I believe it is."

She hardly had a moment alone with Ethan the remainder of the day, which only added to the dreamlike quality of the situation. The entire household went to bed early, anticipating a busy day tomorrow. But when Sara rose to find breakfast nearly ready, and Ethan out doing chores, she found that there was practically nothing to be done except get herself ready. She was sitting at the table when Ethan came in. He gave her one of those endearing grins and said, "Well, good morning, Mrs. Hartford." He winked and added, "That is absolutely the last time I will ever call you that."

Sara laughed softly. "How thoroughly pleasant."

"Amen," Ethan said, and went to the water pump to wash up.

Beyond an occasional reassuring glance from Ethan across the breakfast table, Sara had trouble believing what this day would bring. As soon as she'd finished eating, Mona rushed her upstairs to take a hot bath and shampoo her hair so she could be at her best before the bishop arrived. Soaking for a few precious minutes, Sara silently counted her blessings, then prayed that the rest of her life was going to be as incredibly wonderful as it seemed.

* * * * *

Dressed in the suit that Jon had helped him purchase the previous day, Ethan decided he liked what he saw in the mirror. He actually felt well prepared to become the husband of Sara Brandt Hartford, and he thanked God for blessing him with such unspeakable happiness.

He went to the parlor to find that the furniture had been rearranged, intermixed with chairs from the kitchen so everyone would have a place to sit. The children were dressed in their Sunday best, along with Jon who was sitting with his foot up, reminding the children to behave themselves. Ethan sat down and Phillip climbed onto his lap.

"Are you really going to be my papa?"

"I really am," Ethan said. "What do you think about that?"

"I think it's neat."

"I think it's neat, too," Ethan said. "In fact, I think that being your papa is about the best thing that's ever happened to me."

Phillip grinned. "Are you going to be the baby's papa, too?"

"Yes, I am, and you and me together are going to take very good care of that baby."

Phillip ran to answer the door, then led Dave and Ellie into the parlor, although Ellie quickly disappeared once she'd greeted everyone. Ethan wondered what the women were up to. He felt more anxious than nervous when the bishop and his wife arrived, along with a man they'd talked to in town yesterday. Ethan couldn't recall his title, but he knew that he'd brought the marriage license and some legal book wherein he'd record the event. A few minutes later Maddie's parents arrived, and Ellie returned to the room with Baby Anne in her arms. Ellie and Maddie's mother fussed over the baby, and Ethan impatiently wondered when they would get the thing started. A few minutes later, Maddie and Mona came in and sat down, and he realized that everyone was here except Sara. He was ready to stand up and go find her when she walked into the room, taking his breath away. He immediately rose to his feet, and everyone else did the same. She wore a flowing white dress that made her appear almost angelic. Ethan knew, from hearing the women talk, that she had borrowed it from Maddie; it was the dress Maddie wore to the temple. She also had white silk flowers pinned into her dark hair. She looked more beautiful than he'd ever seen her as she stepped toward him and put her hand in his.

Ethan held Sara's gaze while his mind focused on the words of the ceremony. The vows were exchanged with firm conviction, and their marriage was sealed with a kiss. He marveled that something so brief and simple could have such a profound effect on their lives. They exchanged embraces and handshakes with everyone present, Jon being the last to approach them after he'd sent the children to change clothes before they ate. He embraced Sara, saying, "I am so happy for you, sister."

"Thank you," she said with tears in her eyes.

"And you," Jon said, firmly shaking Ethan's hand. "I'll be proud to call you my brother, but I still expect you to see to the chores until I get back on my feet."

"Yes, sir," Ethan said and Jon gave him a comical scowl. "My brother," Ethan added, and they exchanged a firm embrace.

Ethan enjoyed listening to the dinner conversation while they shared a fine meal. Mona and Maddie had worked to prepare the main dishes, and Ellie and Sylvia had brought along additions. He felt too caught up in the joy to say much himself, and Sara's silence made him wonder if she was feeling the same way. She often met his eyes and smiled, but somewhere in the middle of dessert he caught her gaze and held it, attempting to fathom the actuality of the step they'd taken. They were practically strangers. They were husband and wife. But the prospect of getting to know her better every day made the future seem like a glorious treasure hunt.

The day passed by quickly as their company stayed on and visited, and then Dave and Glen insisted on doing Ethan's chores before they went home. Ethan found it odd, as the day came to a close with family prayer, that it almost seemed as if nothing had changed. Except that *everything* had changed. After Phillip had been tucked into bed in Hansen's room, Ethan walked Sara to her room, just as he'd done the last two nights. She laughed when he carried her over the threshold, then he set her down and their eyes met for the hundredth time that day. His heart quickened. He wanted desperately to stay with her, but he felt he had to say something.

"Listen . . . Sara . . . I know this has all happened very quickly, and with the baby coming and all, well . . . if you're not comfortable with me staying here with you, I can sleep in the next room until after the baby comes and—"

She looked appalled and astonished. "Is that what you want, Ethan?" The question had a subtle bite and he wondered if he'd unintentionally insulted her.

He took her shoulders into his hands and looked at her hard. "I want to be close to you every minute of every night and day. But I don't want to put you in a position where you feel you—"

"I want you to stay with me, Ethan," she said, her voice now soft with pleading. She eased into his arms. "I'm so tired of being alone . . .

of being lonely. I want you to hold me through the night. I want to wake up in your arms."

"Yes, ma'am," Ethan said. She saw the understanding in his eyes, and he closed the door behind them.

* * * * *

For the first time since he'd come to live with the Brandts, Ethan didn't want to get out of bed. He woke with the cock's crow, but observing his beautiful wife, sleeping in the predawn light, he felt so overcome with awe that he could hardly move. In spite of having to get up and see that the animals were cared for, he was still glad they'd waited to have a honeymoon until after the baby came. Not only did Jon need his help, Sara didn't feel well enough to be traveling. And she hadn't wanted to leave and have any trouble come upon the family while she wasn't around to help solve the problem. Still, being here with her, in a life where he'd become more than comfortable, seemed like honeymoon enough to him.

Ethan did his chores and returned to find the bed still warm and Sara sleeping. He snuggled close to her back and wrapped his arm around her while he softly kissed her cheek. She moaned in protest, then with pleasure when she realized it was him. "You're a scoundrel, Ethan Caldwell," she teased, and rolled over to face him.

"Yes, I am," he declared proudly. "And you, Mrs. Caldwell, are more beautiful now than I've ever seen you."

She smiled and said, "If you keep saying things like that, Ethan, you'll never get rid of me."

"That's the idea, isn't it?"

"Yes," she said and kissed him, "I do believe that *is* the idea. Oh," she added, "I forgot to mention . . . I was quite impressed with how well you signed your name on our marriage certificate. And it's a very elegant signature, I noticed."

"Thank you," he said proudly. "Mrs. Humphrey, the woman who took me in . . . I told you about her?"

"Of course."

"Well, she told me she didn't have the patience to teach me to read and write, but she insisted that I learn to sign my name. She said it was something important that I would need to be able to do. And she made me practice it a great deal."

"Well, I can't wait until you learn to write everything in such an elegant hand. I will be expecting long, adoring love letters from you that I can tuck in a drawer and show to our children one day."

Ethan laughed pleasantly at the idea. "I love you so much, Sara. And did you know I picked you up at the train station three weeks ago today?"

"Really?" she said. "It's amazing that I could go from being so miserable to so completely happy in so short a time. And I love you, too."

CHAPTER 8
Where Hearts Meet

Sara stayed in bed much of the day, but Jon told Ethan it was normal for her to feel more tired than usual as the end of her pregnancy drew closer. And she had kept very busy the last few days with all that had been going on. Ethan and Jon drove to town to follow up on some business they had begun two days earlier. Jon had agreed that Ethan's idea would likely give them an advantage, and he was amazed at how easily everything came together.

The following day Sara went into town with Ethan, although they made a point of still behaving like mere acquaintances. Everyone involved had agreed to keep the marriage quiet for the time being. Due to the precariousness of Sara's situation, Ethan felt that if someone came snooping around, keeping them as ignorant as possible might be to their advantage.

After they returned and ate lunch, Sara laid down to rest. Ethan followed her to the bedroom and sat beside the bed. "There's something I need to tell you," he said. She kept her head on the pillow, but focused her eyes on him. "Jon's been helping me with something in town that we finished up yesterday. Maybe I should have talked to you about it first, but . . . well, I kind of wanted it to be a surprise."

"Yes?" she said eagerly.

"Well, here it is," he said, handing her some papers.

Sara sat up and took them. She glanced over one sheet, and then another. "I'm too tired to read all of this right now, and I don't understand," she said.

"Well, if someone does come after your money, then—"

"*Our* money," she corrected.

"Very well, *our* money. Anyway, if they do, they can't take what's been spent. There is the deed to the property you wanted to buy, and the other is a contract, paid in full, for a house to be built there." She laughed, and he added in a silly voice, "And you'll notice your husband's elegant signature at the bottom of those papers."

"Yes, that part I noticed," she said, and put her arms around his neck. "Thank you, Ethan. It was a wonderful idea."

"Peter Carter, the builder, said he could get started on it as soon as the worst of winter gets past. Jon said he could probably put up with us until it gets built."

"What a relief," Sara said, hugging him tightly.

On Sunday they all went to church together, and Ethan wondered how life could feel so much the same and be so thoroughly different. They received some speculative glances from people who noticed they were holding hands, but he didn't care. For all these people knew they were simply courting—which he figured they were, in a way. Even though she had his name, they were still courting as far as he could see.

They had only been home a few minutes when a knock came at the door. Ethan was the closest to the door and went to answer it. His heart quickened with dread when he saw a stern-looking man on the porch. He was dressed in a way that made Ethan relatively certain where he'd come from, even before he said with a thick Boston accent, "I'm looking for Mrs. Sara Hartford. I understand this is where she's staying."

"Who wants to know?" Ethan asked, doubting that a criminal would come to the front door and ask to see her.

The man pulled open his coat to reveal a law badge. He said, "My name is Lincoln Saunders. I'm a detective with the Boston City Police Department. Mrs. Hartford spoke with me about some concerns before she left. I wonder if I could have a word with her. I've come a long way."

"Yes, you certainly have," Ethan commented, and opened the door for him to come in. "Why don't you have a seat there in the parlor and I'll go and get her."

"Thank you," Mr. Saunders said as Ethan closed the door.

Ethan found Sara sitting at the table. "There is a Mr. Saunders from Boston here to see you."

"Good heavens," Sara said, coming to her feet. Maddie looked alarmed. "It's all right," Sara explained. "He's the detective I spoke with following Harrison's death." Maddie nodded and Sara turned to Ethan, "Stay with me."

"Every minute," he answered and followed her back to the parlor.

"Mr. Saunders," Sara said, entering the parlor, "I certainly didn't expect to see you here."

"I figured it would be a surprise," he said, extending a hand. "How are you settling in?"

"Very well, thank you," she said, accepting his handshake. "I see you met my . . ." She hesitated. "Uh . . . this is Ethan Caldwell."

The two exchanged a handshake and all found seats. "So, I must ask," Sara began, "what brings you all the way out here? It must be serious if you've come this far and invested so much time."

"Well," he said, "admittedly, I have been putting a great deal of time into the case surrounding your husband's death; however, I must keep my suspicions confidential for the time being. Let's just say I have a strong lead, and I felt it was important to come here personally and make certain that you were well."

"Oh, yes," she said. "I'm doing very well."

They discussed her situation, and Sara came around to the point where she felt comfortable telling Mr. Saunders about her marriage. He seemed pleased with the circumstances, and agreed that it could very well help keep Sara and her assets protected. When Mr. Saunders informed them that he planned to stay in the area for a few days to keep an eye on things, Sara asked, "Do you mean to imply that whoever is responsible might be around here?"

Cautiously he said, "I believe it's possible, but I can't know for certain."

Sara told him of the telegram she'd received, which only seemed to add to his conviction that he should stay close by for a while.

"You must stay and have dinner with us," Ethan said.

"Yes, you must," Sara echoed. "You won't find any place around here to buy a meal on Sunday. In fact, do you have a place to stay?"

"I confess that I don't," he said. "I came straight from the station. I was hoping you could suggest a place."

"Well, there isn't much around here," Sara said. "But we have an extra room. You'd be welcome to stay."

Mr. Saunders smiled, and Ethan decided he liked him. It was easy to see that he had Sara's best interests at heart, and his concern was genuine.

Jon, Maddie, and Mona all gave Mr. Saunders a warm welcome. The dinner conversation was delightful as the group shared their experiences of growing up in Boston. Ethan gained a new perspective when he discovered that Mr. Saunders had actually come from a background of poverty, and struggled to get an education. He now realized that coming from Boston didn't necessarily mean an upper class background.

The meal was nearly finished, and the children had gone upstairs to play, when there was a knock at the door. Mona rose to answer it as Mr. Saunders said, "I would lay odds on that being your attorney, Mrs. Caldwell."

"Geoffrey?" she almost squeaked. "What on earth would he be doing here? And how would—"

The detective smiled, saying, "We ran into each other on the train. We had a number of long chats during the journey. Apparently he's come out here for the same reasons I have. We made a little wager on who might get here first. I would bet that Mr. Warren had more trouble finding a ride from the station than I did."

Sara rose to follow Mona, then apparently had second thoughts and took her seat again. They could hear Mona greeting a gentleman at the door and Sara said softly, "It *is* him." She laughed. "I can't believe it."

Mona brought Geoffrey Warren into the kitchen. By the way Jon and Sara greeted him, he was apparently a long-time family friend as well as their attorney. Geoffrey and Mr. Saunders joked about the wager they'd made on the train, and talked as if they'd become great friends during their journey. Introductions were made, and while the attorney greeted Maddie warmly, he maintained a mildly condescending air toward Ethan. Ethan was glad to at least be wearing his Sunday clothes, but he knew, that for all his efforts, his speech set him apart from everyone else in the room. They offered Geoffrey something to eat, and Mona quickly heated enough food to give him hearty helpings of the meal they'd just finished. Ethan listened to further reminisces of Boston, and was feeling a bit out of place. He was grateful to feel Sara discreetly squeezing his hand beneath the table.

After Geoffrey had finished eating and the conversation turned to the tragedy of Harrison's death, Ethan sensed that Sara was becoming agitated. They were all surprised when Mr. Saunders stood and said, "Well, I thank you for your hospitality, but I really must be going."

"But I thought you were—" Sara began, then stopped abruptly. Ethan felt sure he was the only other person in the room to see the detective's subtle nod telling them to go along with him.

"I'd love to take further advantage of your hospitality, but I really must be running."

Ethan suspected that Mr. Saunders was allowing Geoffrey an opportunity to speak candidly with Sara. Only a minute after he left, Ethan's hunch proved correct when Geoffrey said, "Could we talk, Sara? There's something I need to discuss with you that wouldn't have been appropriate through letters or telegrams."

"Of course," Sara said, but a quick glance in Ethan's direction let him know she felt concerned. Geoffrey and Sara headed toward the parlor. Ethan followed, hovering in the hallway, hesitant to let Sara out of his sight when there was so much to be wary of. He was relieved when she motioned toward him, and he stepped into the room. Geoffrey looked at Ethan with overt disdain, then at Sara, as if he questioned her sanity.

"I want Ethan with me," she stated firmly and sat down.

Geoffrey looked perplexed and annoyed, but he sat across from Sara and started talking in a legal jargon that made Ethan's head spin. Ethan sat and listened, maintaining a straight face that might mask his ignorance. Focusing on Sara, he felt more amazed than intimidated to see her in this new light. Her ability to counter her attorney's every sentence left him in awe. Ethan turned his ear more to the conversation at hand when Geoffrey said, "I think your theory was right, Sara, about Harrison's business dealings. I believe they were connected to his death, somehow. And now the same person—or people—are after that money."

"What are you saying, Geoffrey?" Sara's voice was urgent.

"I'm saying that I've been contacted by the responsible party with a demand for payment of the money Harrison owed them."

Sara exchanged a brief, astonished glance with Ethan, then demanded, "Well, who is it?"

"The contact was made anonymously," he stated.

"Oh, so it's illegal," she concluded angrily.

"Something like that, except that whoever it is apparently has a right to the money."

"A right?" she echoed, even more angry. "Show me some legal document that Harrison signed stating that he owed this money. Show me and I'll gladly pay his debts." Geoffrey said nothing. "You're an attorney, Geoffrey. You should know more than anyone that if it isn't in writing it won't stand up in court. There is nothing legal or moral about what's taking place here, and I am not paying *anyone* for killing my husband and jeopardizing my security."

Geoffrey sighed, seeming more irritated than concerned. "The fact is, this person is adamant in claiming that Harrison owed them a certain amount of money; you are Harrison's widow and heir. His money is now yours, and I think you would be wise to just hand it over. Pay them off. You don't have to give it all up; just enough to get them out of your life. These are dangerous people, Sara. I'm concerned for your safety."

When Sara suddenly smiled at Geoffrey, Ethan wondered if she'd picked up on the same subtle inconsistencies that he had. He instinctively believed that Geoffrey Warren was not what he appeared to be, but he waited quietly for Sara to handle the situation. She'd certainly managed just fine so far.

"Don't you have anything to say?" Geoffrey demanded, his agitation increasing.

"Yes, I do, actually," she said. "You can let this person know—whoever it may be—that pursuing this issue is pointless. I don't have any money, not a single penny."

"*What?*" Geoffrey retorted, erupting to his feet. Ethan did the same, silently daring him to cross an inappropriate line in his anger. But Geoffrey was too absorbed to even notice. "How on earth could you spend that much money in less than a month?"

"Well, I didn't spend anything, actually. I mean . . . my husband bought a piece of ground, and contracted to have a house built, but—"

"What did you say?" Geoffrey interrupted, and Ethan imagined steam coming out of Geoffrey's ears as his face reddened and his fists tightened.

"I think you heard me correctly," Sara said. "I'm married, Geoffrey. You know what that means. There is no way for anyone to lay claim to what no longer belongs to me."

Geoffrey shook his head and laughed dryly. Ethan watched him closely, almost certain that his interest in this was far more personal than he was pretending. "I can't believe it." Then, as if that had given him an idea, he added, "I think you're bluffing. Where exactly is this husband of yours? Surely you have documents to prove this marriage."

"I certainly do," she said. "And Ethan would be happy to show them to you, just before you leave."

Sara rose to her feet as if to dismiss him. Geoffrey turned, looking at Ethan as if he'd honestly forgotten he was there. Ethan figured the timing couldn't be any better to step toward Sara and put an arm around her shoulders. Geoffrey's astonishment couldn't help but make Ethan smile.

"You'd better sit down, Mr. Warren," Ethan said. "You look a little pale."

Geoffrey sputtered angrily toward Sara, "You . . . you married . . . *him?* That's very clever, Sara. What is this? Some name-only arrangement to protect your money? Did you honestly think I would believe you'd—"

"Now you listen to me, Geoffrey, and listen well. I love Ethan more than you could ever comprehend, and he loves me more than Harrison could ever have hoped to comprehend. Now, get out of this house and don't ever come back. If you so much as set foot anywhere near here again, I will see that you are arrested for trespassing. I've said all I have to say to you. Now, get out!"

Geoffrey glared at Sara, then Ethan, then Sara again. He picked up his briefcase and huffed out the front door.

"I do believe," Ethan said, after the door had slammed, "the esteemed Mr. Warren knows more about your first husband's affairs than he's letting on."

"Yes," Sara said, wrapping her arms around him, "I do believe you're right. Perhaps that's what frightens me most of all."

"No need for that," Mr. Saunders said, and Sara gasped as she drew back from Ethan and turned to see him standing in the hall. "Forgive me for being slightly deceptive," he said. "Your brother quietly let me back in the kitchen door."

Jon appeared at his side, and from his expression it was evident he'd also overheard the conversation. Mr. Saunders went on to say, "I wanted to hear what Mr. Warren had to say. The truth is, Mrs. Caldwell, I came all this way because our investigation led to Geoffrey Warren, and I've been tracking him. When I got wind of his plans to travel here, I made certain I was on the same train."

"Good heavens," Sara said and teetered slightly. Ethan guided her to the sofa and sat beside her. Jon sat down and set his crutches aside.

Mr. Saunders sat across from them and continued his explanation. "Given Mr. Warren's agitation in the conversation, combined with evidence that I won't bore you with, I believe we have our man."

"Are you saying . . ." Sara hesitated, as if she couldn't bring herself to voice what she was thinking.

Jon said firmly, "That *is* what you're saying, isn't it? Geoffrey killed Harrison."

Mr. Saunders answered calmly. "I doubt he did it personally. But I am relatively certain he's directly involved with whoever it was. I have a partner who came out with me, although he's remaining incognito and we've had no direct contact. He's following Mr. Warren's every move. If it's all right with you, I'll stay here tonight and head out in the morning on the east-bound train, which I believe is what Mr. Warren will do. Now that he knows there's no way of getting to your money, I suspect he'll just go back to Boston and try to let the dust settle. We are absolutely certain that Mr. Warren came alone. We've been watching him very closely. If he attempts to return here in the meantime, my partner will be right on his tail, and we'll know if he gets anywhere near the house."

Sara sighed audibly, and Ethan could see how upset she was even before she said, "I just can't believe it. When I think how we've trusted him, and . . . I just can't believe it."

"It's incredible," Jon said, the anger in his voice evident. "But I still have trouble understanding what exactly took place. Now that we know Geoffrey was involved, can you tell us what you know?"

"Well," Mr. Saunders sighed and scratched his face thoughtfully, "after putting all that we could gather together, we figure that Mr. Hartford had the opportunity to invest in an illegal business deal. It was very risky, but very lucrative."

"What exactly do you mean, Mr. Saunders?" Sara asked carefully.

"We haven't been able to pinpoint it exactly, but we are relatively certain it had to do with smuggling opium into China."

"Good heavens!" Sara gasped and put a hand to her heart.

"Forgive me," Ethan said at the risk of sounding terribly ignorant, "but what exactly is opium?"

Without sounding the least bit condescending, Mr. Saunders explained, "Opium is used in many pain-killing drugs. I'm certain your brother-in-law makes good use of opium-based drugs in his medical practice. But it's very addictive if it's used over a long period of time. Addiction to opium has been a huge problem in China, and it's been illegal there for many years, so it's a valuable commodity when smuggled into the country. We believe that Mr. Hartford invested a large sum of money in an opium shipment, hoping for high returns, but the ship was apprehended leaving India, where the goods had been acquired, and the cargo was confiscated. Hoping to get back the money he lost, he tried again, but this time he borrowed the money, not wanting to sell any of his assets or upset the household. When trouble happened a second time, he couldn't possibly repay the loan without alerting you to the problem, since money would need to be drawn from accounts that you kept track of. But we're not certain what made him so hesitant to come clean and pay the debt; he must have known that the people he was dealing with weren't ethical by any means. While we can't be absolutely certain, we believe we've had problems with these people before. They loan money with exorbitant interest rates, and they respond to lack of returns with violence."

"I can't believe it," Sara said, her eyes distant. "How could he be such a fool?"

"How could he believe he'd get away with it?" Jon asked.

Sara's response was angry at first, and then hurt. "Oh, he was arrogant enough to think he could get away with just about anything. But as difficult as he was to live with, I find it disturbing to think that he would put us—and himself—in so much danger." She sighed, then looked to Mr. Saunders and asked, "What could have possibly prompted him to get involved in such a thing?"

"Surprisingly enough, there are many businessmen who get into such things. For some people, money is something they just can't get enough of. We believe Mr. Warren is the direct link between the smuggling operation and the people who loaned Mr. Hartford the money. Now that we have sufficient evidence to have him arrested, we're hoping he'll be the pawn we need to get to the bottom of this."

"We're grateful to you, Mr. Saunders," Jon said. "I must say we've been terribly concerned. Knowing you're here gives us some added peace of mind."

"I'm glad to help," he said. "And if all goes well, I can be back in Boston and have all of this settled in time to share Christmas with my family."

Ethan was surprised to hear the holiday mentioned. He'd been vaguely aware of the children's excited chatter about it, and Jon and Maddie had occasionally mentioned something of their plans, but Ethan had been too caught up in his life changes and concern for Sara. Now that the problem was nearly settled, the idea of sharing Christmas with his new family took a more prominent position in his mind.

They had a pleasant visit with Mr. Saunders through the evening, and the night passed without event. Ethan drove the detective to the station early, thanking him again for his help. Mr. Saunders promised to let them know how it all turned out. "Stay alert," he said to Ethan as they shook hands on the platform. "You can never be sure, but I really think there's nothing to be concerned about."

"Thank you again," Ethan said.

"My pleasure, and . . . Oh, I wanted to say, I'm genuinely pleased about your marriage. She's a good woman, and I'm glad to see her so happy."

"You and me both," Ethan said.

* * * * *

The holiday officially began when Ethan took the children in the sleigh to cut down an evergreen for the Christmas tree. While Mona and Maddie were cooking and baking, and the children were stringing popcorn and making paper decorations, Sara mostly sat and observed. He had noticed that she'd suddenly reached a point in her pregnancy where she was terribly uncomfortable. Her face bore signs of swelling, as did her feet, which she kept propped up most of the time. At Jon's suggestion, Ethan rubbed them for her at least three times a day, which she declared eased the ache in them immensely.

Ethan kept busy caring for Sara and Jon while everyone else worked at Christmas preparations. He often teased, "The two of you would be in a fine pickle if it weren't for me. Look at you, both sitting around with your feet up, as if you didn't have a care in the world."

"Yes, you're right," Jon said one particular day, "we *would* be in a pickle without you."

"Some of us more than others," Sara said with an affectionate smile. A moment later she jumped and laughed.

"Getting kicked?" Ethan asked, and she nodded.

He leaned forward from rubbing her feet and pressed his hand over her belly. She guided his fingers to the appropriate spot and they laughed together when it happened again. Ethan was excited at the very idea of his involvement in the forthcoming birth of this child. He already felt as if it were his child, and the life he'd found with Sara was the greatest thing that had ever happened to him. He could see now that while his marriage to Hannah had been good and they'd been happy, there was something undefinably different in the feelings he shared with Sara—something he'd never felt before. And that's where the fear came in. As the end of her pregnancy drew closer, he couldn't help wondering what he would do if he lost her the way he lost Hannah. Could he live through another ten years of groping his way out of the gutter, battling the loneliness and guilt? He knew that to have such thoughts destroyed faith, and he did his best to pray for her safety and put it out of his mind. He just had to believe she would be all right.

For Ethan, Christmas unfolded around him in a way that seemed almost dreamlike. He'd always appreciated Christmas and what it meant, but he'd never imagined that it could be so filled with the Spirit, so full of love and unity. At moments he almost felt that it was too good to be true. And he could only hope that this was just the beginning of all they would share through their lifetimes.

Three days after Christmas, a telegram arrived from Lincoln Saunders. Geoffrey Warren had been arrested and was being held pending a trial. He confessed to a certain amount of involvement when he'd realized he was cornered, and they were attempting to bargain with him for information on others that were involved. While the news evoked poignant feelings on the part of the family members who had trusted and liked Geoffrey for most of their lives, Sara admitted that she felt immensely relieved to know it was almost over. Later that day she went into labor.

Ethan sat by her bedside, holding her hand in his and fighting to keep his nerves from showing. Jon assured him several times that the pain was normal and everything would be all right, but he found it difficult to believe. He helped pass the time, for himself and Sara, by talking about the house they would build. "And we'll have a beautiful stable with a big corral where we can keep a couple of fine horses. And we'll go riding together, and we'll take the kids on picnics in that patch of trees at the east end of our property. And we'll grow the most beautiful garden you've ever seen, and when we irrigate it, we'll walk between the rows barefoot and squish the mud between our toes."

Sara smiled at him between pains. "Keep talking, Ethan. When you run out of things to say, start over."

Ethan did just that, talking and holding her hand as afternoon moved into evening, and evening into night. The pains became more powerful and closer together, and he had to fight to keep his wits and distract her. Jon periodically checked on her and reported that all was well. Maddie and Mona took turns coming in to see that all was ready for the delivery. Ethan just prayed that it would be over soon, and that she would be all right.

When Sara neared the end and the pain became constant, Ethan held her so tightly that he feared she would break. For hours she groaned and cried and dug her fingernails into his arms. And when he felt certain that neither of them could bear another second, she gasped and collapsed in his arms. He heard Jon chuckle just before he declared, "It's a girl, Sara. She's perfect."

Ethan laughed as Sara clutched onto him tightly, laughing through her tears. Maddie wrapped the baby in a little white blanket and set her in Sara's arms. Ethan couldn't hold his own tears back as he observed his tiny new daughter. And yes, he felt completely as if she were his own.

"Congratulations . . . Papa," Jon said, slapping him lightly on the shoulder.

"Same to you . . . *Uncle,*" Ethan said and together they laughed.

"Oh, she's beautiful," Sara said, touching the little face.

"She looks like her mama," Ethan added, touching Sara's face. She looked up at him and he finished, "I'm so proud of you, Sara."

She reached up to touch him and said, "I couldn't have done it without you, Ethan. I love you more than life."

"Amen," he said and kissed her.

Jon hobbled back to the chair he'd been sitting on to deliver the baby. Ethan had seen enough animals born to know that it wasn't completely over when the baby came. He wasn't surprised when Sara moaned and grimaced for a moment, although it was nothing compared to her expressions of pain a few minutes ago. And he was grateful to have Jon there, and to know that Jon knew what he was doing. But Ethan's gratitude caught in his throat when he heard Jon say in an alarmed tone, "Hold it! Whoa."

"What is it?" Ethan demanded, but Jon ignored him.

He saw the color drain from Sara's face as she moaned again.

"Maddie, take the baby!" Jon ordered. "Mona, hand me that . . . that . . . yes, thank you."

Ethan kept his focus on Sara's face, trying to shut out the panic in Jon's voice that filtered through the pounding of pulse beats in his ears. Sara groaned and gazed at Ethan with a fear in her expression that matched his own. She cried out as if she'd been stabbed. Ethan glanced to the side only long enough to see Jon's hand, covered in blood, pressing hard on the sheet that covered Sara's belly.

"I've got to stop the bleeding, Sara," Jon said, forcing a calm voice, as if to explain why he was causing her pain. A moment later he muttered, almost under his breath, "Dear God, help me."

Ethan felt the nightmare of losing Hannah begin to swirl around him. Images of her dying in his arms clouded into his mind until he found it difficult to focus on Sara's face. He felt snapped out of a daze when she murmured in a voice that was barely audible, "I love you, Ethan. You've made me . . . so happy."

Ethan watched her eyelids flutter closed. "No!" he groaned and held her tightly, recalling the way Hannah had done the very same thing. "Don't you die on me! Do you hear me? I can't live through this again. I can't!"

When she didn't respond, his breathing became so sharp that he feared he'd pass out.

"Maddie!" Jon shouted. "Get Ethan out of here—now!"

"No!" Ethan protested.

"Ethan!" Jon shouted. "Now, you listen to me. She's my sister and I want her to live every bit as much as you do. But I can't do what I have to do to save her life with you in here. Now get out of here and let me get on with it."

Ethan took a longing gaze at Sara, doubting he would ever see her alive again. He numbly allowed Maddie, who was still holding the baby, to escort him to the kitchen where he slumped into a chair.

"I knew it," he muttered, hanging his head. "I just knew it."

"And what do you think you knew?" Maddie questioned, sitting beside him.

"I knew I just didn't have enough faith to keep her here. If only I had believed more. If only I hadn't given into my fears and—"

"Is that what you think faith is?" she demanded in a voice that got his full attention. "Do you think God somehow measures how much faith we have and decides whether to punish or reward us accordingly?"

Ethan looked dumbly at her, realizing she'd summed up how he'd been feeling, but to hear it expressed that way made it sound so much more ridiculous than it had seemed in his head.

"Now, you listen to me, Ethan Caldwell! That's Satan talking through your hat! Do you hear me? That's not how it works at all." Her voice softened and she put a gentle hand on his arm. "Faith is trusting in the Lord, Ethan, and accepting His will. Yes, we have to pray for our desires. And yes, He hears our prayers and answers them, but the answers have to be according to His will. It was Hannah's time to go, Ethan, and no amount of faith or prayers could have saved her. If it hadn't been her time to go, God would have provided the help she needed. Now Sara's life is on the line. We both know that, and it's frightening. But God is not going to punish us for being afraid, Ethan. Yes, He wants us to trust in Him, and through that trust we can find peace. But we have to accept that it's in His hands and we have to find peace with whatever He gives us. Now, you've got one of the best doctors in the state in there with her. He's going to do everything in his power to save her. But you've got to accept the possibility that she might not make it."

Ethan sucked in his breath and barely managed to keep from sobbing. "But you listen to me." She moved her face closer to his and took both his hands into hers. "Whether Sara lives or not, you will always have the love she gave you. She made you a part of her family. We all love you and need you, Ethan. You have a place with us, forever. But most important, you have two children now who need you to be a father to them whether Sara makes it or not. And you must never forget that most precious gift our Savior gave us to help us get through when His will is so very difficult to accept. The Atonement will carry your sorrow, Ethan, and it can also compensate for the faith we don't have when we're just not strong enough to make it through. So don't you start feeling sorry for yourself and forget how much you have to give. Just be grateful for all that you've been given. It's hard, I know it's hard. But whatever happens, we'll get through it together. Do you hear me?"

Ethan nodded firmly and realized that he actually felt better. Afraid, yes. Inadequate, yes. But Maddie's words had allowed a measure of peace to penetrate his frightened and aching heart. He could see a tiny glimmer of hope against an otherwise black sky, and under the circumstances, any hope at all could go a long way.

"Are you going to be all right?" Maddie asked.

He nodded again, but a moment later the emotion flooded into the open. He hung his head and sobbed like a lost child. Maddie eased her arms around him, letting him cry until there were no more tears left. As his cries ceased, the house became eerily silent. He wanted to go upstairs and demand to know what was going on. He wondered if Sara had actually died and Jon was simply dreading coming to tell him. He closed his eyes and prayed with all his heart and soul that she would come through this ordeal and be able to share her life with him. And as difficult as it was, he prayed that if it was God's will for her to be taken now, that he would be able to stay strong and be a good father to the children she had left in his care.

Ethan's prayer was interrupted when the new baby began to fuss. Maddie stood to pick her up and Ethan watched through dazed eyes as she held the baby to her shoulder and gently patted her. The baby settled immediately and a moment later Maddie was putting her into Ethan's arms.

"She needs her father," Maddie said, and left the room.

Ethan cried a different kind of tears looking into the face of his beautiful little girl; she looked so much like her mother. He truly was blessed. He'd gained so much in comparison to what he'd lost with Hannah's death. And he would live in gratitude for his blessings. He would live to honor Sara and the love they shared, whether she was by his side or not. But, oh how he prayed she would live!

"Ethan," Jon said, and he turned, startled. He wondered how it was he didn't hear Jon hobbling down the stairs and into the room. His heart pounded. He held his breath. Jon's face was completely unreadable. Was the hint of moisture in his eyes a result of grief or joy? He was about to scream, demanding that Jon tell him, when Jon added quietly, "She's fine. Everything's under control."

Ethan slumped with relief and held the baby closer, weeping into the blanket she was wrapped in. He felt Jon's hand on his shoulder and put his own hand over it.

"She's asking for you, brother."

A burst of laughter erupted from Ethan's throat as he shot to his feet. "Thank you, Jon," he said, and hurried up the stairs. Only the fact that he was holding the baby kept him from running. He stepped tentatively through the open bedroom door to see Mona, looking haggard herself, straightening up the room. He barely caught a glimpse of blood-soaked rags in a basin before he turned his focus to Sara. Her eyes were closed, but he could see she was breathing and he inhaled as if he could drink in the reality that she was alive and real.

"Thank you," he said, and her eyes came open.

She smiled weakly and asked in a raspy voice, "For what?"

"For staying around."

She reached a hand out for him. He laid the baby by her side and sat on the edge of the bed, taking her hand in his. "I love you, Ethan," she said, and his vision blurred with new tears.

He bent over to carefully take her into his arms, crying tears of joy into her dark hair strewn over the pillow. "Oh, and I love you," he said.

"Ethan," she said, and he could feel her hand in his hair. He straightened enough to look into her eyes. "I want to name her Hannah . . . only if that's all right with you, of course."

Ethan laughed and readily agreed. "It's perfect," he said and touched her face. *"Everything* is absolutely perfect."

She smiled again and he kissed her.

* * * * *

Just after the new year, a letter arrived from Lincoln Saunders. Jon read it aloud over lunch, after the children had gone off to play. Sara held Ethan's hand tightly as she listened to the facts being laid out. Geoffrey Warren had been convicted of his crimes, along with two other men involved in the scandal. Geoffrey had confessed everything upon condition of a lighter sentence. The information he gave up brought the ringleader to light. It seemed that Geoffrey had been involved with shady business deals for many years. He had initially urged Harrison to invest in the smuggling operation, and then mediated between Harrison and those who loaned him the money. Apparently Geoffrey received a large percentage of the interest for arranging such loans and seeing that they were collected. Geoffrey had not been responsible for Harrison's death, but he was well aware of the ensuing investigation it would cause; therefore he had no choice but to give Sara time to get settled in Utah before pursuing her with the hope of getting his returns. Mr. Saunders finished his letter by saying: *I'm pleased to tell you that Mr. Hartford's killer has been convicted and is awaiting a sentence. I wish you the best in your new life, and will always fondly recall my visit to your home.*

"Well, I'm sure glad that's settled," Jon said, putting the letter back into the envelope.

"So am I," Sara agreed, feeling the relief envelop her. She hadn't realized how thoroughly the problem had weighed on her until now—now that it was completely over. She turned to look at Ethan, baby sleeping against his chest, and she silently thanked God for blessing her life so completely. She had never imagined that she could be so happy. But Ethan smiled at her, and she knew it was reality. She was just plain happy.

Epilogue

Sterling, Utah—1906

"All right. All right. I'm coming," Ethan said, laughing as he attempted to dodge the three little ones hovering at his feet. He almost spilled the milk and eggs in the buckets he held in each hand.

"I've got this one," Phillip said, taking the milk bucket from him.

"Thank you, son. Your mother wouldn't appreciate us losing the milk over a little impatience."

He finally stepped ahead of Hannah and her little brothers and hurried into the house—all three of them running after him.

"Oh, finally," Mona said, taking the milk from Phillip. "I can't get the cake finished without this. Thank you, my boy. Now get along upstairs and get cleaned up. Your cousins will be here in half an hour for the party."

Ethan set the bucket of eggs down and paused to absorb the serenity he was feeling. He'd finally come to accept that his happiness was not too good to be true. Each and every day Sara's love for him and the children, and her mere presence in their home, proved to him just how true it was. And everything that had been good for them had gotten better when he'd been blessed with the opportunity to baptize her. They'd finally gone to the temple to be sealed a few months before the twins were born.

He momentarily ignored the impatience of the children and moved stealthily behind Sara where she stood at the stove, stirring something that smelled incredible. She laughed when he wrapped his arm around her from behind and pressed his lips to her throat.

"I can't get this dinner on with you distracting me like that," she said. He chuckled and kissed the other side of her neck. "You're a scoundrel, Ethan Caldwell."

"Yes, ma'am," he said, tightening his embrace. "And you, my dear, are beautiful."

She laughed. "I must admit I look a lot better than I did two years ago."

"Well, being pregnant with twins may not have put you in your best form, but you were still beautiful."

"You're very sweet, Ethan, but everyone will be here soon, and I have a lot to do. Could we pick up this conversation later . . . after the children are all asleep, perhaps?"

"I'll be counting on it," he said, and stepped back. "So, what can I do to help?"

"The best thing you can do is keep the little ones occupied until we get dinner on."

Ethan felt a tug on his leg, and they both looked down to see Hannah—who was now three and a half and the spitting image of her mother—along with her twin brothers. Each one held a story book, and they were staring at their father with pleading eyes.

"All right. All right. Come along," he said, and led the way up the hall to the front door. They went onto the porch where they could enjoy the summer evening. Ethan sat in the center of the porch swing, settling Hannah on one leg and the twins side by side on the other.

"Mine first. Mine first," they all cried simultaneously, and he laughed. Engaging in a familiar ritual, he closed his eyes while they held their books in the air, vying for the most likely place he would grab at. He reached out and took the first one he got his hands on. The other two were set aside, and he opened the first to begin reading.

"Oh, I like this one," he said. "It says here that it's about the three billy goats gruff. What does the goat say?"

"Baaa!" they all bellowed in unison.

Ethan laughed and began to read.

The End

ABOUT THE AUTHOR

Anita Stansfield has been writing for more than twenty years, and her best-selling novels have captivated and moved hundreds of thousands of readers with their deeply romantic stories and focus on important contemporary issues. Her interest in creating romantic fiction began in high school, and her work has appeared in national publications. *When Hearts Meet* is her eighteenth novel and sixth historical work to be published by Covenant.

Anita lives with her husband, Vince, and their five children and two cats in Alpine, Utah.